Is Death the End of All Existence or the Gateway to a New Life?

This question has dominated man's thinking from the beginning of time. Searching for an answer, philosophers speak of heaven and hell, reincarnation, or spirit worlds beyond our Earth. But, ultimately, only the dead can know the truth. How then can we hope to discover whether there is, indeed, some kind of existence after death and what such a new form of being is really like?

Drawing on the experiences of people who have been pronounced clinically dead only to be miraculously revived, the case histories of men and women who have actually participated in the phenomenon of astral projection, and the reports of witnesses who have observed spirit manifestations, Martin Ebon explores all the data on this fascinating subject, creating a compelling and provocative case for the new life that awaits us beyond the limitations of our physical bodies.

The Evidence
for
Life After Death

By Martin Ebon

A SIGNET BOOK
NEW AMERICAN LIBRARY
TIMES MIRROR

Copyright © 1977 by Martin Ebon

First Signet Printing, August, 1977

1 2 3 4 5 6 7 8 9

 SIGNET TRADEMARK REG. U.S. PAT. OFF. AND FOREIGN COUNTRIES
REGISTERED TRADEMARK — MARCA REGISTRADA
HECHO EN WINNIPEG, CANADA

SIGNET, SIGNET CLASSICS, MENTOR, PLUME AND
MERIDIAN BOOKS are published in Canada by The New
American Library of Canada Limited, Scarborough, Ontario

PRINTED IN CANADA
COVER PRINTED IN U.S.A.

Acknowledgments

The author is indebted to a number of specialists, researchers and colleagues for their kind and generous cooperation in making this book possible. Among them are Dr. J. B. Rhine, Foundation for Research on the Nature of Man; Dr. Karlis Osis, Chester Carlson Research Fellow, the American Society for Psychical Research; Mr. W. G. Roll, Project Director, the Psychical Research Foundation; Mr. Stuart Blue Harary, Division of Parapsychology and Psychophysics, Maimonides Medical Center; Mr. John W. White, author and editor; Mr. John R. Egle, Mockingbird Books, Inc.; Dr. Robert Crookall, researcher and author; Mr. D. Scott Rogo, researcher and author; Ms. Grazina Babusis, Librarian, The Eileen J. Garrett Library of the Parapsychology Foundation, Inc.; the Hopkins Marine Station, Stanford University, Pacific Grove, California; Mrs. Betty Mahoney, Spiritual Frontiers Fellowship, Baltimore.

Sections from *Life after Life,* by Raymond Moody, Jr., reproduced in the chapter "The Moody Phenomenon," are reprinted by permission of the publisher. Copyright © 1975 by Raymond A. Moody, Jr.

Contents

"There is only a single supreme idea on earth: the concept of immortality of the human soul; all other profound ideas, by which men live, are only an extension of it."
—Fyodor Dostoevsky (1821–1881),
  in *Diary of a Writer*

The Evidence
for
Life After Death

1. Alone with Your Soul

Do you have a soul?

Can it separate from your body?

Will your soul survive your body's death?

These questions have been asked ever since man became aware of his identity, ever since we've known that death awaits the baby from the moment it is born.

Have we become too squeamish to ask such simple, yet so deeply penetrating questions? Are we too self-assured, too modern or too cynical, or possibly too cowardly, to come right out and ask these questions, and seek the answers?

If you are one of those cynics or cowards, don't read on; put down this book and walk away. But what, exactly, are you trying to walk away from? From death? From reality? From the possibility or the reality of life after death?

If death is not the end, if it is only a gate to an existence beyond life as we know it, why are we so uncertain about it all? We *are* squeamish about death, for all our permissiveness on virtually all other subjects that were taboo a generation or two ago.

Oh yes, we have learned to postpone death. In fact, we seem to have learned it all too well. At this very moment, large numbers of old people, and some young ones, shut away in nursing homes, hospitals and private homes, are little more than wilting weeds. Modern medical science has extended their lives, day upon day, week upon week, month upon month, and year upon year for what? To preserve a human being from an end to suffering? Or to prevent a soul from crossing over into another level of existence, a life after death?

All these are crucial questions. If there is life beyond death, medicine has no need to use what are currently called "extraordinary means" to postpone what may clinically be called life but bears little resemblance to a state of living. If

1

there is life beyond death, and our daily rounds are merely a preparation for another and presumably higher existence, doesn't that give a more profound meaning to this life we are living today?

The doctrine of reincarnation, which teaches that ours is just one in a chain of many lives, makes good sense. It explains much that seems unjust in our life and the lives of millions of others on our planet. Reincarnation could give new meaning: with each life, each rebirth, an improvement over a previous existence is achieved. Finally, perhaps, we move on to a higher sphere, no longer physically visible on this earth plane under normal conditions, but possibly able to return to it, or to influence the lives of those who live here in positive or negative ways.

The idea of life after death is encumbered by a tradition that speaks of ghosts and demons, of darkened séance rooms and mysterious mediums. Right now, this concept is the target of various categories of scientific investigations which seek to ignore much that has gone before and seeks to solve the riddle of death by novel means. Simply put, these modern scientists proceed much like a lawyer who must prove a case for which no direct evidence can be firmly obtained, but who can marshal much evidence that is "circumstantial." This means that the lawyer must bring to the trial witnesses and exhibits that can prove his case by indirection, but nevertheless strong and numerous enough to convince a jury; some fields of science, such as biology, use similar methods.

And that is precisely the role in which those who seek to establish the existence of life after death find themselves today. We have tried for about a century, certainly since the establishment of the Society for Psychical Research in London in 1882, to prove the survival of the human personality after death, by such means as spirit voices in séance rooms, interrogations of apparitions, the use of "automatic writing" which may originate with discarnate entities—all this, and much more. But as scientific proof, as direct evidence to convince "the jury"—ourselves—this accumulation has fallen short of its goal.

However, in just about the last decade, breakthroughs have taken place that put new findings into the category of circumstantial evidence for life after death.

Let me give you two ways of looking at this approach, odd

as they may sound initially. First, you may remember reading H.G. Wells' book *The Invisible Man*, or perhaps you've seen the movie on the Late Show. Well, in this story there is a double difficulty, for the moviemaker and those who are trying to trap the "Invisible Man"—they have to make him visible by getting his outline somehow, by throwing something over his elusive form, such as a sheet or a net. It has to come from the outside and create, as it were, an illusion of visibility. This is eventually what happens: the "Invisible Man," invisible no longer, is trapped and bound.

Our next metaphor is that of a hunt. To track down and establish an elusive scientific phenomenon—which is what "life after death" is to researchers—is very much like the hunt for a powerful but elusive, and perhaps only legendary, animal, something like the Loch Ness Monster or the Unicorn. When, in the summer of 1976, scientists from the United States invaded Loch Ness in Scotland, they approached the legendary creature from all sides, with all the gadgetry of modern science, in order to gain at least as much as a radar impression of the creature. They did not, but they will try again.

Similarly, and this is my third metaphor, reporting on events inside Mainland China has in recent years best been done from its fringe, from the outside: radio broadcasts, newspaper and official press reports, together with stories told by travelers and escapees, have formed a mosaic to create a picture which, after Chairman Mao's death, proved to be remarkably accurate.

If all these comparisons seem far-fetched and, given our context, a bit odd, remember that we are dealing with something elusive and invisible, possibly legendary, perhaps purposely hidden, and certainly quite remote from our normal cognitive powers. We have difficulty enough understanding foreign languages or even everyday gestures. All through the Near East, where we would signal "no" with a shake of the head, Greeks, Turks, Arabs and others give a quick raise to their heads and click their tongues. In India, people shake their heads lightly from side to side, in situations when we would be nodding in agreement.

Trifles? Yes. But indicative, by their microscopic nature of the macrocosm we are dealing with, of the huge gap between our habitual thought patterns and the world-beyond-our-world that any investigation of life after death must seek to fill.

How, then, are modern researchers clothing the "Invisible Man," and from what directions and by what means do they hunt the elusive creature, or gain knowledge of a secrecy-shrouded country?

Like the hunter, the parapsychologist who studies afterlife seeks to encircle his target, to draw closer and closer and at the very least get a good glimpse of it. On occasion, death, from which no traveler returns, does permit a man or woman to enter briefly, look around, and pull back rapidly enough to gain some quick insight. Increasingly, people who have been declared clinically dead have been brought back to life, resuscitated, and have lived to tell of their experience. Their stories are remarkably similar. They have, for the most part, come back with a feeling of strength, of a more positive view of life—and of death.

And then there are those who have moved outside their bodies while alive. They are the soul travelers, or, to use the technical term, those who have had an Out-of-the-Body Experience (OOBE, or OBE for short). These experiences used to be quite spontaneous, and they overlap with those who have been clinically dead but returned to life. Someone placed on an operating table whose heart has stopped functioning, might find himself floating over his own body, looking down on the doctors working to save his life. Similarly, someone in an OBE condition, but quite well, may find himself floating away from his body and seeing or hearing all kinds of things, while being an "Invisible Man" to everyone else in the room or even outside the room.

It is not easy to fit these and related research methods into the framework of twentieth-century scientific techniques. The big gap is between colorful case histories and science's standard demand for the repeatable experiment. The same gap exists between a single strong laboratory result, for example in an out-of-the-body test, and the now-traditional requirement for hundreds or even thousands of tests that provide a broad enough basis for statistical evaluation.

Parapsychologists today are trying hard to establish links between spontaneous and laboratory results. At the same time, they are building bridges between related, but nevertheless separate concepts. For example, take the idea that something we call the soul is the element that survives the body's death. Well, then, if we can establish that something soul-like exists within or aside our living body, isn't it fair to assume that it is this very soul which later on survives the dead body? That is but one bridge-building hypothesis.

Another hypothesis states that parapsychologists have established that there are people who are gifted with telepathy (reading other people's minds) and clairvoyance (able to view events remote from them, but not through someone else's mind). Thus, while mediums have claimed that spirits of the dead have spoken to them, and told a sitter things that only she or he could know, these mediums might simply have been reading the sitter's mind. Skeptics say that this doesn't prove that a spirit was present, or that there's life after death, but merely—although that's plenty—that the medium is a good telepath. How, then, can you separate telepathy and clairvoyance, on the one hand, from spirit communication on the other hand?

It was this dilemma that prompted Dr. J.B. Rhine, the most prominent parapsychologist in the United States, to abandon research into life after death in the 1930's, saying that he couldn't tell whether a medium was giving them spirit communication or practicing ESP (extrasensory perception, which includes telepathy and clairvoyance). One of Dr. Rhine's associates, Dr. Karlis Osis, undertook ESP experiments which suggested a fading effect of telepathy at a distance. However, he calculated, if a spirit communicator were involved, there would be no such fading. Pushing the concept a step further, he set up a worldwide network of mediums who were instructed to "tune in" on a communicating spirit at a given time, with allowances made for time differences around the globe. He set out to obtain fragments of communications from each medium, to be fitted together later on into a coherent pattern of words and sentences. He called this a "linkage experiment," becaused it linked the mediums together, and he worked with other researchers who organized and recorded experiments in various parts of the globe. The experiment was so designed that it could give statistically valid results.

As you can see, modern researchers have gone to great lengths and used ingenious experimental designs and hypotheses to make the invisible into something not only visible but scientifically acceptable. In doing so, they had to give up the

original hope of psychical researchers of the second half of
the nineteenth century, and much of the first half of our own
century. That hope and aim had been: direct, convincing and
scientifically acceptable communication with spirits. Séance
room techniques had been moved into a laboratory environment, or at least been subjected to laboratory-like controls.
Cheating, whether conscious or unconscious, had to be ruled
out. Experimenter bias or emotional involvement had to be
curbed. Designs and evaluations of tests were subjected to increasingly careful scrutiny.

One way of eliminating human error was the effort to construct a machine designed to contact the dead. As I noted in
my book *They Knew The Unknown*, the fabulous inventor
Thomas A. Edison had very definite ideas along these lines.
He told his friend B.C. Forbes, founder of *Forbes* magazine,
the business periodical, about his plans, and these were published under the title "Edison Working to Communicate with
the Next World" in *The American Magazine* (October,
1920). Edison reflected the same views in his personal diary.
His train of thought was expressed this way:

"If our personality survives, then it is strictly logical and
scientific to assume that it retains memory, intellect, and
other faculties and knowledge that we acquire on this earth.
Therefore, if personality exists after what we call death, it's
reasonable to conclude that those who leave this earth would
like to communicate with those they have left here."

Edison added that he was "inclined to believe that our personality hereafter will be able to affect matter." He also said:
"If this reasoning is correct, then, if we can evolve an instrument so delicate as to be affected, or moved, or manipulated
... by our personality as it survives in the next life, such an
instrument, when made available, ought to record
something." But he didn't think that séance room devices
were appropriate. Rather, he said, "Certain of the methods
now in use are so crude, so childish, so unscientific that it is
amazing how so many rational human beings can take any
stock in them. If we ever do succeed in establishing communication with personalities which have left this present life, it
certainly won't be through any of the childish contraptions
which seem so silly to the scientist."

Later, in an article on Edison published in *Liberty* magazine, a close acquaintance of the inventor, Allen L. Benson,

confirmed that Edison had "wondered whether it might not be possible to make a machine that would enable the hereafter to prove itself without the aid of mediums or other living human agencies." This is precisely what a worldwide group of researchers are presently trying to do. Some are working individually on sophisticated, special devices; others, and their number runs into the hundreds, now seek to record spirit voices on tape, quite independent of what Edison called "mediums or other living human agencies."

Before closing this introductory chapter and reporting in greater detail on today's circumstantial approach to life after death, I want to add a few personal words. By now, I have been active in the field of parapsychology for well over two decades. I spent twelve of these years in close association with Mrs. Eileen J. Garrett, the medium whose performance prompted Dr. Rhine to give up his laboratory inquiry into survival of the human personality after death and to concentrate entirely on ESP. In the course of these years, I have attended hundreds of séances, encountered a vast variety of psychic sensitives and scientists concerned with life after death, while building up a fairly strong immunity against what can be a dangerously attractive fascination with "those other worlds."

But I am, of course, not immune to the eternally tempting question, "Do we live after death?" Like so many others who later moved into less emotion-oriented work or who even turned into skeptics or militant antagonists, my first fascination was with the afterlife question. I well remember my first visit to a medium, the late Frank Decker, who then lived in an apartment off New York's Central Park West. It was a hot summer day, I traveled by subway to Decker's place, and I was understandably nervous about the whole undertaking. During the sitting later on, an entity addressed me in an apologetic and even contrite manner, speaking of his grave error in having denounced a certain "Margery" and saying that now, as he was "on the other side," he had changed his mind about spirit life and was trying to make up for the mistakes he had made earlier.

The whole thing meant nothing to me. Only years later, when I had become familiar with the history of physical research in the United States, did I realize that the spirit entity who was seemingly addressing me had identified itself as

Dr. Walter Franklin Prince, one-time Research Director of the American Society for Psychical Research (ASPR) and, during an interim, of the Boston Society for Psychic Research. In this capacity, the usually quite skeptical and at times even acerbic Dr. Prince investigated the mediumistic phenomena around "Margery" Crandon, who achieved fame and notoriety and virtually broke up the ASPR; her role remains controversial to this day. Harry Houdini, the magician, was one of those determined to expose her, and the "Margery" case won nationwide, even worldwide publicity.

I knew nothing of this while I was sitting in the dark in Frank Decker's apartment. The name "Margery" rang no bell with me. But when one of the entities told me that I had been needlessly upset on my way to the séance, I was startled. Surely, only I could have known my subway state of mind, this mixture of eagerness and unease that I had brought into the Decker apartment. Certainly, the medium might have sensed my attitude. But, young and inexperienced as I was, I was quite impressed.

Naturally, I observed Eileen Garrett in trance states many, many times, and I carried on hour-long conversations with her two spirit controls: the "Keeper of the Gate," Uvani, and Garrett's main trance personality, Abdul Latif. Many of Mrs. Garrett's friends and fans were irritated by her public reluctance to accept the validity of life beyond death. She had been a practicing medium for over forty years, but she put off her admirers by saying to them, "Well, perhaps Uvani and Abdul Latif are nothing but splits off my own personality. Who can tell?" I used to tease her by saying that she believed in an afterlife on Mondays, Wednesdays and Fridays, was a cool skeptic on Tuesdays, Thursdays and Saturdays, and on the seventh day she rested! At this, she would smile and say something appropriately enigmatic. I urged her, before I left the Parapsychology Foundation in 1965, to give a definitive answer to this often-asked question about her true belief about life after death, at least in her final book. She did write the book, *Many Lives* (1967), but it did not settle the question; she died in 1970, taking the answer with her.

I think that Eileen Garrett was totally sincere in her attitude of hope and doubt. She would surely have welcomed today's efforts to get at the eternal question by novel means of research. Unable to give a definitive answer herself, she had established her foundation, at least partly to give scientists the means to engage in research that would provide a definitive reply, once and for all.

Well, perhaps we are now on our way!

2. Man's Ultimate Search

Contact with the dead, ancestor worship, and the idea that there is an existence beyond death, may well be the origin of all religious thought. One of the earliest documents available, the Babylonian tablets of *The Epic of Gilgamesh*, deals with a search that leads the protagonist into a shadow world of the dead, where he pleads for an answer to the question, "Why must man die?" In his masterful work *The Golden Bough*, Sir James G. Fraser suggests that, when early man dreamed of the dead, he believed he was in actual contact with them. In ancient Greece and Rome, numerous devices for speaking with the dead, much like the Ouija board of today, were in use.

A common heritage, Shamanism, can be found in Alaska, Siberia and southern Asia. A Shaman is a male medium, and his trances and contacts with a world beyond our own, are used in other civilizations by "witch doctors." In Africa, Brazil and Central America, trance practices that link the living with the dead, or with divinities (these terms are almost interchangable) are alive today.

Are these attempts to communicate with the dead mere primitive superstition? Or do preindustrial societies intuitively understand that man is immortal? In England, during the Victorian Era, these questions were posed at a time when science, industry and technology were making rapid strides which threatened established beliefs. The writings of John Stuart Mill on the philosophy of science had alerted the public to a new appreciation of the scientific method. Charles Darwin's *The Origin of Species by Means of Natural Selection* had been published in 1859, and his work had a profound influence on Western culture. His evidence, demonstrating that man had slowly evolved from a more primitive creature, had all but countermanded popular religious beliefs about creation. The public began to lose faith in such religious tenets as divine creation, immortality and resurrection during this time, and Church attendence slackened considerably. At the turn of the century, science was all-important. People were losing interest in dogma and theology. If Man survives death, they contended, it would take more than the Bible's promise to make them believe it. The intellectuals of the day wanted scientific evidence. And it was at this time that several philosophers, psychologists and physicists embarked on a search to collect empirical evidence that Man survives death.

The first organized attempts to collect this evidence were made in Great Britain and were due, to a great extent, to the labors of a group of Cambridge philosophers. Chief among these were Professor Henry Sidgwick, the "father of English philosophy"; F.W.H. Myers, his pupil; and Edmund Gurney, a philosopher and scholar. All of these men were fascinated by the problems of religion. (They were all three the sons of clergymen.) But they also realized that such beliefs as immortality and resurrection had little scientific merit. Instead of losing faith totally, though, they decided to search for empirical evidence which could be used in support of Christian doctrines. They soon turned their eyes toward an odd American cult which had recently caught on in Europe. Ever since the 1850's, Spiritualism had been the rage of Europe; it taught that man could directly contact the dead through psychics, at séances, and that the dead could directly contact the living either through apparitions, through hauntings, or telepathically. Sidgwick, Myers and their colleagues decided that, if properly investigated, Spiritualism might be able to offer scientifically acceptable evidence of survival after death.

In 1882, these scholars joined forces with several Spiritualist leaders to found the Society for Psychical Research (SPR). The goals of the society were to investigate all aspects of psychic phenomena, sift out fraud and self-delusion from genuine reports, employ strict standards of evidence during this quest, and publish their findings. Although the SPR studied considerably more than just those phenomena which indicated post-mortem survival, several of its original founders, most notably F.W.H. Meyers, were primarily interested in this deeply emotional question of afterlife.

At first, the SPR founders collected and studied cases of spontaneous psychic experiences, and in 1886, Gurney, Myers, and Frank Podmore published a collection of these cases, entitled *Phantasms of the Living*. It was a tome of some 1,300 pages, complete with reports of telepathy, apparitions and premonitions. The volume dealt only incidentally with evidence for life after death. Another survey, undertaken in 1889, was designed to confront this central issue more directly. In that year, the SPR circulated a questionaire throughout Great Britain which merely asked:

"Have you ever, while believing yourself to be completely awake, had a vivid impression of seeing or being touched by a living being or inanimate object, or of hearing a voice, which impression, so far as you could discover, was not due to any external physical cause?"

The SPR received answers from 17,000 people, of which 2,272 were in the affirmative. What surprised the researchers was that no less than three hundred or so correspondents reported having encountered apparitions. In eighty cases, the apparitions were recognized by the viewers as someone who had just died or who died shortly thereafter. (These cases were dubbed "crisis apparitions." A crisis apparition was defined as one which appeared either twelve hours before or after the death of the person seen.) Of these eighty cases, thirty-two were well-evidenced. For example, the viewer may have told someone about seeing the apparition before he learned of the agent's death himself. In ten cases, the SPR substantiated that the viewers did not expect, nor had any reason to suspect, the death of the agent. A report on the survey was published in 1894 as a *Report of the Census of Hallucinations*. Here is a typical case which was included in their report, and which was sent to the SPR in 1890 by a Mrs. G. Adeleine Baldwin based on her life in India:

"I was my Uncle E de C.'s favourite niece, and we had made a compact that whichever of us died first should appear to the other. I was about 25 at the time, and he said to me, 'You won't be afraid, but, if God permits such a thing, I will come to you.' This took place in Camareah, in 1860. I was then a widow, living at my uncle's house. It was in December 1863 (I had married again and was living at Umritsur), when one morning at about 4 o'clock, as I was sitting up in bed with my baby in my arms, I saw my uncle. He was laying on the sofa in the drawing-room and appeared to be dying. I also saw his bearer and my aunt's ayah. They passed each other in going across the room, and looked at me and sighed. I said to my husband, 'Look, there is my uncle dying,' and I described the above scene. He thought it so remarkable that he got out of bed and made a note of it. He wrote at once to my cousin C., to inquire after uncle, and we heard from him that my uncle had died very suddenly, on the day and at the time I saw him, of heart disease, after an illness of four days, at his house in Mirzapore."

This was just the kind of evidential case which interested the SPR. There was an independent witness to the story (Mrs. Baldwin's husband, who had made note of the incident); the uncle, to the best of Mrs. Baldwin's knowledge, had not been in failing health; and the uncle died in his home, just the way the percipient had seen him.

Other cases reported in the *Census of Hallucinations* are no less interesting. One man reported to the Society in 1891 that, when he was stationed in India, he had awakened one night to see the figure of his father—who was still in England—by his bed. "Goodbye, Jim, I won't see you any more," it said. A few weeks later the correspondent received a letter informing him that his father had died at exactly the time of his experience.

These cases are thought-provoking, to say the least, but did they really indicate that Man will survive death? The SPR founders had mixed opinions on this issue. Edmund Gurney, who had been the principal author of *Phantasms of the Living,* did not think so. Gurney, long interested in telepathy, believed that crisis apparitions were a form of telepathic communication. He argued that apparitions are not really physical objects at all; instead, he maintained, they are telepathic hallucinations. He theorized that the viewer probably received a telepathic impression of the death unconsciously. The unconscious mind they created an hallucination of the dead person, in order to transfer the information into consciousness. Gurney pointed out that apparitions usually appear dressed in normal clothing, are sometimes seen by only one person and not by anyone else in the same room, and even walk through walls! These factors hardly indicated that apparitions were genuine, physically present spirit entities.

F.W.H. Myers, on the other hand, pointed out that some apparitions were seen collectively—that is, observed by more than one person at the same time. He felt that some element of the dying person's mind was actually visiting the viewer and making its presence known. Therefore, he argued, apparitions do indicate the capability of the mind to survive death.

Gurney countered by reasoning that a person seeing an apparition might telepathically infect others in the room with him so that they, too, would see the figure. Myers retorted that there was no evidence supporting this theory. These arguments went round and round, and were never really resolved.

However, the SPR researchers soon began focusing their attention on a phenomenon which could serve as stronger evidence for survival after death: apparitions seen years after death of the agent (post-mortem apparitions). In fact, by the 1890's, the SPR had collected more than 370 such cases. In some of the reports, the apparitions even communicated information to the percipient which the latter had not previously known, such as directing him to lost wills. One of the most famous of these cases is called "the scratched cheek case" because of the peculiar evidence the apparition afforded.

The case was reported by a Mr. F.G. (His real name was not disclosed) whose sister had died of cholera when only eighteen. F.G. saw her apparition some nine years later during a business trip to St. Joseph, Missouri. He was resting in his hotel room when he suddenly had the impression that someone was in the room with him. Glancing around, he was shocked to see the lifelike figure of his long-dead sister standing before him. The apparition was disfigured, though, by a long red scratch on its cheek, but it said nothing and faded from view. F.G. reported his experience to his parents as soon as he returned home. Much to his amazement, his mother admitted that, while helping dress the body for burial, she had accidentally scratched her daughter's cheek. She had carefully hidden it with makeup and, in shame, had never told anyone of the little accident.

Can this case be explained by telepathy? If so, telepathy from whom? From the dead sister? Or the mother?

Even though the SPR amassed a great number of post-mortem apparition cases, whether or not they served as proof of man's immortality was an issue they left unresolved. However, Edmund Gurney realized that such cases, especially when the apparition conveyed information, could not be explained by his telepathy theory. Myers, on the other hand, was firmer in his beliefs and felt that the evidence for the existence of post-mortem apparitions did prove life after death.

Around 1890, SPR researchers began to turn their attention away from ghosts and apparitions in order to concentrate on a new and excitingly different avenue of research. As I pointed out earlier, the SPR founders were very interested in Spiritualism, which had migrated to Europe from the United States. Mediums abounded, claiming that they could tip tables with the aid of the spirits, communicate with the dead, materialize their figures, and generally engage in dialogues with the dead. Most of these phenomena were phony; fraud and credulity were rife. The SPR leaders investigated scores of mediums, but found that few were worth studying.

All this changed in 1885, when the eminent American psychologist-philosopher William James communicated to the SPR that he had found a remarkable trance medium in Boston, Mrs. Lenore Piper. James had visited the medium incognito, yet she had gone into trance and "brought through" several of his deceased relatives, who correctly gave their proper names, relationships, etcetera. The SPR was impressed by James' report and sent one of its top investigators, Richard Hodgson, to investigate Mrs. Piper. Hodgson's job was simple: verify the woman's abilities, or expose her.

Hodgson, an especially critical investigator, took complete control of Mrs. Piper's séances. He arranged them and wouldn't allow her to know who her sitters were. In fact, he asked Mrs. Piper to go into trance before her sitters even entered the séance room. Nevertheless, as soon as Mrs. Piper became entranced, another personality took over her body: he called himself Dr. Phinuit, claimed to be a French physician and spoke with a French accent. Phinuit offered to bring through the departed relations of the sitters, and he seemed to do just that.

For example, at Hodgson's own first sitting, Phinuit correctly described some of Hodgson's deceased relatives. He tried to bring through one particular relation, but could only say that the name began with the letter R. Hodgson had a deceased sister named Rebecca. Phinuit proceeded to mention the name "Fred" and added, "He says you went to school together. He goes on jumping-frogs and laughs. He says he used to get the better of you. He had convulsions moments before his death struggles. He went off in a sort of spasm. You were not there." Hodgson verified that all this information was absolutely correct. He had indeed had a school friend named Fred who was a jumping-frog whiz. The information about his death was also correct.

But Phinuit wasn't finished yet. He proceded to discuss details concerning Hodgson's relationship with a woman who had been his fianceé. Then Phinuit declared that she was present.

The good doctor also had a propensity for the quietly melodramatic. Hodgson once arranged for a Mr. Robertson James to have a séance with Mrs. Piper. During the sitting, Phinuit announced to James that his Aunt Kate had just died and joined him in the spirit world. This message didn't impress James, whose aunt was ill but very much alive at the time. However, returning home, he found a telegram waiting for him announcing his aunt's death.

In order to investigate Mrs. Piper's abilities more thoroughly, Hodgson and the SPR leaders decided the medium should travel to Great Britain. There the sittings could be conducted under totally controlled conditions, giving the medium no possible chance to "check up" on her sitters. The SPR leaders could make sure that she had no opportunity to learn who her sitters were going to be. They would keep her under strict surveillance and make sure that everyone who attended her sittings were strangers to her. With this in mind, Mrs. Piper sailed for England in 1889.

The SPR experiments were held under tight control. Nonetheless, Phinuit still had no difficulty in bringing through intimate information about the SPR investigators' departed relatives. Sir Oliver Lodge, one of the society's leaders and one of England's most eminent physicists, had an entire series of sittings with Mrs. Piper. For one test, he handed Phinuit an old pocket watch which he had borrowed from his Uncle Robert especially for the séance. As soon as Phinuit touched the watch, a voice shouted through the entraced medium, "This is my watch, and Robert is my brother, and I am here. Uncle Jerry, my watch." The entity went on to describe many of his boyfriend adventures: risking being drowned in a creek while swimming with his brothers, killing a cat in a boyhood haunt called Smith's field, owning a snakeskin, and other minor memories. Lodge was amazed. The watch he had handed to Mrs. Piper really had belonged to his dead Uncle Jerry. On writing back to his Uncle Robert and to another relative, Lodge was able to verify everything Mrs. Piper had communicated. Phinuit even gave him intimate information about the death of his father.

Despite the obvious accuracy of Mrs. Piper's psychic abilities, the SPR leaders were still far from convinced that they were in direct contact with the dead. Hodgson, for instance, thought that Mrs. Piper's abilities had nothing to do with communication with the dead. He believed that, instead, when in trance, Mrs. Piper telepathically tapped the minds of her sitters in order to gain all the information she needed. He went on to argue that her subconscious mind then assembled this information and built up secondary personalities who merely imitated the sitter's relatives. Actually, Hodgson's theory did help explain many peculiarities about Mrs. Piper's mediumship. For example, Phinuit had given information about his own life in France, but SPR investigators couldn't verify any of it. When Phinuit was told that his story hadn't panned out, he changed it! He couldn't even speak French very well. Sometimes the information he gave about a sitter's deceased relatives turned out to be totally incorrect. So, many psychical researchers studying Mrs. Piper just couldn't believe that Phinuit was really a spirit, and preferred to think he was some split-off portion of the medium's own mind. Lodge and Myers, on the other hand, were duly impressed by Mrs. Piper's abilities, and both came to believe that the medium was in direct touch with the dead.

Piper's mediumship underwent a profound change: she de-
Even Hodgson eventually changed his mind. In 1892, Mrs.
veloped automatic writing and began to give her communications in writing instead of through her voice. (In fact, during one phase of her career she could simultaneously give communications from two different entities; one using her voice, the other writing through her hand.) A new "control" (the personality who runs the séances as Phinuit did), named George Pelham, gradually replaced Phinuit as the chief communicator; and this personality was bound to have a profound influence on Hodgson's attitude toward the Piper case.

Pelham had, in life, been an old chum of Hodgson's. He had even promised to return from the grave and communicate to his old friend if he possibly could. And he did just that. Over the next several months, Pelham communicated hundreds of details about his life to Hodgson. Old friends of Pelham's were introduced into the séance room after Mrs. Piper had become entranced. Invariably, Pelham would recognize these persons, call them by name, tell of his relationship to them, even calling them by nicknames he had used when alive. Hodgson eventually wrote a second report on Mrs. Piper in which he gave up his telepathic theory and admitted his belief that the entities who communicated through Mrs. Piper were just who they claimed to be: the dead.

Despite Hodgson's conversion, many leading psychical researchers of the Victorian Era still believed that telepathy and clairvoyance could account for the type of information mediums such as Mrs. Piper brought through. They believed that a medium could tap not only the client's mind, but the mind of anyone in the world; and the debate between those who accepted the survival hypothesis (the survivalists) and those who rejected it (the anti-survivalists) soon became totally deadlocked.

However, a different type of mediumistic evidence indicating survival became apparent in Mrs. Piper's automatic writing, and in the work of other mediums the SPR had discovered after the turn of the century. Myers had died in 1901, other SPR founders also died around this time. And gradually, the SPR leaders, still working with Mrs. Piper and other mediums, decided that the personality of Myers was trying to communicate with them through several different mediums. These messages went on for months. Those in charge finally realized that Myers was giving only part of his messages through one medium, while giving the rest through one or two others. The messages only made sense when the parts were joined together. These jigsaw puzzle messages were especially intriguing. Often, the communications, when pieced together, alluded to classical literature, history, and mythology. These were topics with which Myers was fully conversant during his life, but beyond the education of many of the mediums he was apparently using as his channels. These scripts, known as the cross-correspondences, and became exceedingly intricate. It seemed that Myers, still interested in the SPR's work, wanted to provide evidence which was more complex and harder to dismiss than most mediumistic communications.

For example, in 1906 Myers communicated the themes of death, sleep, shadows, dawn, evening and morning through the automatic writing of Mrs. Holland, one of the SPR's mediums who lived in India. About this same time, Mrs. Piper spoke while coming out of trance, "Morehead—laurel for Laurel. I say give her that for laurel. Goodby." Mrs. Piper also saw the apparition of a Negro. The next day, while entranced, she stated that a key to understanding this cryptic message could be found by examining some automatic writing produced by Mrs. A.W. Verrall, another SPR psychic. This same direction had been given in Mrs. Holland's scripts. Obviously, Myers was planning a cross-correspondence. During the next month, Mrs. Verrall's daughter wrote automatically, "Alexander's tomb—laurel leaves, are emblem, laurels for the victor's brow." Mrs. Holland subsequently communicated, "Darkness, light, and shadow, Alexander Moor's head." Another medium communicated the words, "Dig a grave among the laurels." None of the SPR's psychics had contact with the others, nor had they any way of knowing what was being communicated in their colleagues' scripts.

Now, it is obvious that all these messages were interrelated. However, they make little sense to today's readers. But they *did* make sense to the SPR leaders, who were well versed in classical history and literature. The key to these cryptic messages came to them months later when yet another one of their psychics, Mrs. Willett, communicated, "Laurential tomb, Dawn and Twilight." It became clear that all of these messages referred to the tombs of the Medici family. The laurel was the emblem of Lorenzo the Magnificent. Other symbols on the tombs represent Dawn and Twilight. The name "Alexander" refers to Alessandro de Medici, called "The Moor" because he was mulatto, and so forth.

What can we make out of the cross-correspondence? Several SPR leaders felt that some external will was obviously directing the communications. They thought that the personality of F.W.H. Myers had indeed survived death and was proving his existence by masterminding an ingenious plan. Other researchers were less sure. They argued that all of the SPR mediums might be in telepathic rapport, "sharing" information with one another. The debate over the evidentiality of the cross-correspondence still goes on today, but perhaps one of the most cogent evaluations of the scripts has been written by the eminent contemporary British parapsychologist Dr. Robert Thouless. As he states in his book, *From Anecdote to Experiment in Psychical Research:*

"If this was an experiment devised ... on the other side of the grave, I think it must be judged to be a badly designed experiment. It has provided a mass of material of which it is very difficult to judge the evidential value, and about which there are varying opinions. It reproduces, in fact, the defects of spontaneously gathered mediumistic material in a some-what intensified form. A successful experiment should give a more clear and unambiguous answer to the question it is designed to answer than does spontaneous material; otherwise the experiment is not worthwhile. When judged by this criterion the cross-correspondences would seem to fail as an experiment."

Nonetheless, efforts prove survival of death by working with mediums did not stop after Mrs. Piper retired. This type of research went on just as strongly from the 1910's to the 1940's. In fact, stronger evidence was procured by psychical researchers in the 1920's and 1930's, when several SPR and independent investigators began to work with another medium, Mrs. Gladys Osborne Leonard, who became known as the "English Mrs. Piper."

One of Mrs. Leonard's primary investigators was a British clergyman, the Reverend C. Drayton Thomas. Thomas was fascinated by the possibility that survival after death could be proven experimentally, but he was also quite aware that te-lepathy from the sitter could account for much of the in-formation that mediums usually come up with. So, for some of his tests with Mrs. Leonard, he devised what he called "proxy sittings," in which he would try to contact a discar-nate entity whom he had never known on behalf of another party. For instance, he might try to contact the departed wife of a friend. After contact was made, he turned the records of the séance over to his friend for evaluation. Thomas' plan was to separate the medium as much as possible from the person to whom her communication would be addressed, hoping that this procedure would counter the argument that the medium merely taps the sitter's mind during a séance.

A good example of a series of proxy experiments is the "Bobbie Newlove Case," which Thomas published in the *Proceedings* of the SPR in 1935. In 1932 Thomas received a heart-rending letter from one Herbert Hatch, who hoped that, through Mrs. Leonard, the clergyman could get in touch with his little ten-year-old grandchild, Bobbie, who had died of diphtheria. Thomas was doubtful that a ten-year-old child would make a good communicator, but he wrote back to Hatch saying he would try.

Eleven séances were held in an attempt to contact Bobbie. The boy had little difficulty communicating through the medium and babbled on about a dog-shaped salt shaker he had owned when alive. Usually though, Bobbie did not communicate directly, but gave the information to Feda, Mrs. Leonard's control, who repeated it to Thomas. Bobbie and Feda also communicated information about a sandwich-board poster costume he had once worn, about an injury to his nose, and even gave correctly the name of the street which bordered his school. Finally, Bobby tried to offer some information about his death, blaming the illness on some pipes near his school. The message didn't make much sense at first, but it was eventually discovered that Bobby liked to play around some pipes on a hillside near his school. The pipes dripped water into stagnant pools, and apparently Bobby had become ill after drinking the water.

Though Thomas' proxy experiments are interesting, they cannot serve as watertight evidence that we live after death. After all, if a medium can tap the mind of the sitter, why not the mind of a person hundreds of miles away? There is even some evidence that this type of super-ESP occurs during mediumistic séances.

In 1921, S.G. Soal, the top British parapsychologist, started experimenting with Mrs. Blanche Cooper, a prominent London medium, who gave séances at the headquarters of the British College of Psychic Science. Soal's basic plan was to get in touch with his deceased brother, Frank. The experiments were going just fine until one day his brother spoke through the medium, "Sam. I've brought some one who knows you." Soon after, Soal got the shock of his career when a distantly familiar voice greeted him. "Well, Soal, I never expected to speak to you in this fashion," it said. Soal couldn't place the voice until the communicator added, "Remember Davis—Gordon from R–R–Roch–Roch." Soal interrupted the voice in his excitement and exclaimed, "By Jove, and it's like Gordon Davis too."

As he wrote in his report, the voice he heard was identical to the one Davis had possessed in life, as far as he could remember. Gordon Davis was an old school chum who, Soal believed, had been killed in the war; and during the next several séances, Davis communicated to Soal such information as the name of the school they had attended, details of their last conversation, and even described the furnishings of his earthly house. It was a great case, evidentially speaking.

But then, quite some time later, Soal received a double shock. He discovered that Davis was very much alive and living in London. In fact, he had been engaged in a business transaction at the exact time his "spirit!" had first greeted Soal at the Cooper séance. Soal could only conclude that somehow Mrs. Cooper had telepathically picked his mind, and possibly Davis' as well. But the investigator was in for an even ruder shock. While investigating the Davis matter, and meeting up with his old friend after years of lost contact, Soal learned that Davis had not yet furnished the house in which he lived at the time of the Cooper séances. Yet, the medium's description of the furnishings did match how the house was eventually decorated. In other words, Mrs. Cooper had used precognition to determine how Davis would later decorate his residence.

The Gordon Davis case, published in the *Proceedings* of the SPR in 1925, dealt a death blow to much mediumistic evidence. The case seemed to prove, once and for all, that mediumistic investigations and communications—no matter how evidential—could never prove life after death. Even today, fifty years later, few parapsychologists believe that mediumistic evidence will ever resolve the survival controversy. Even though there are cases on record which tell how mediums spoke in languages they had never learned, or who wrote automatically in the exact handwriting of a person long dead, parapsychologists have all but abandoned this type of research to explore the possibility of life after death.

During the maturation years of psychical research, there were some highly ingenious independent attempts to prove Man's immortality. After all, psychical research and Man's search for proof of immortality, was not the sole province of the SPR. For example, in 1907 a Boston physician named Duncan MacDougall published a report which chronicled his attempts to weigh the body at death. As he explained in his report, "Hypothesis Concerning Soul Substance, Together with Experimental Evidence of Such Substance" (which was published in the May, 1907 issue of the *Journal of the American Society for Psychical Research*): If the soul survives death and resides in the body, then it should maintain weight. And if the soul departs from the body at death, the body should show a sudden loss of weight at that exact moment.

To test his theory, MacDougall enlisted the aid of several terminal tuberculosis patients. Each of them was placed on a delicate scale when death was imminent, and over the course of several experiments MacDougall discovered that, at the exact moment of death, the bodies of his subjects inexplicably lost a couple of ounces. The ejection of air from the lungs, or the evaporations of sweat off the body could not account for the readings.

MacDougall carried out his research at Massachusetts General Hospital, where he was employed. No one has ever come up with a normal explanation for his results, but the physician had to abandon his experiments because of public pressure and outrage over his "immoral" research.

Meanwhile, in Europe, Hyppolite Baraduc, a French psychical researcher, attempted to photograph the body at the time of death. He hoped that he might be able to photograph some ethereal substance which left the body at that time, and he was able to procure and publish several photographs showing orbs of light floating about his wife's body after her death. Again, no one has ever fully explained these photographs.

The early psychical researchers were the first intellectuals to examine scientifically and test the possibility of the survival of the soul. However, their work was a mixture of success and failure. On the one hand, they proved that Man's mind houses many psychic potentials. They also proved that a large body of circumstantial and experimental evidence exists which indicates the possibility that the human personality survives the death of the body. But on the other hand, they were never able to prove this possibility. There were too many complicating factors at hand. However, the first psychical researchers did pose many questions about Man and his soul which researchers are still trying to answer. They established a pattern which today's experimenters seek to adapt, improve, and advance.

3. The Moody Phenomena

Ivor Potter's motorcycle had crashed, and he was taken, unconscious, to a nearby hospital: "I woke in the hospital to feel myself floating out of my body," he recalled later. "I was surrounded by a golden light." This is not the impression of a man easily given to spiritual fantasy: Potter, a telephone engineer, is as down-to-earth a person as you'd ever be likely to meet. He added, "I kept going upwards until I reached a beautiful garden in a peaceful land. There was a range of blue mountains in the distance."

These events took place when Potter was 26 years old. He now recalls his experience as "the most marvelous feeling," that he just "wanted to keep going." In this setting, away from his own unconscious body, Ivor Potter encountered his father—a man killed in a road accident, only two weeks earlier—who admonished him, "Go back; you have your mother and sister to care for."

Potter says he returned to his body reluctantly, but reconciled himself to this return when he found his mother and sister crying at his bedside. The physician in attendance, he recalls, "said I was almost a goner."

And what has this experience done to Potter, a man now 48 years old?

"I used to be scared of dying," he says. "Now the only thing that worries me is doing all the things I have to do while I'm alive."

Ivor Potter's story is the first one in this chapter, because it gives his full name, cites his profession, and tells where he lives: in Bude, Cornwall, England. Many accounts of such out-of-the-body experiences are published anonymously, presumably to protect those who tell them from embarrassment. At other times, they are simply broken down into categories and become dry statistics.

It was the work of a man who has collected some 150 such

stories, Dr. Raymond Moody, which prompted people like
Potter to come forward and tell their own experiences, and
which almost precisely parallel those Moody accumulated.
Potter, and dozens of others, reported their OBE's in a London newspaper, *The Sun.* The specific experiences and lasting
impact of these near-death events are about as identical with
the American cases that Moody collected, as anything like
that can be. Floating experiences, encounters with departed
relatives, and an end to fear of death are among the themes
Moody encountered over and over again.

That Dr. Moody's collection should have such a swift
transatlantic response is characteristic, I think, of the positive
manner with which Moody lifted the dark veil of something
heretofore as unspeakable as the death experience. Men and
women, by the thousands, have lost their reluctance to tell of
these striking impressions, no longer afraid they might be
called peculiar of fanciful.

Ever since he published his book, *Life after Life* (Atlanta,
1975), Moody has traveled widely, speaking to thousands to
whom he has brought not only a series of fascinating stories
but a feeling of buoyancy and reassurance. In his writing, as
well as in his public and private appearances, Dr. Moody en-
courages an easy confidence, a candor that prompts men and
women to confide in him as they have not confided in anyone
else in their lives. I discussed these "Moody phenomena" with
an old friend at a luncheon club in Washington, D.C., early
in 1977. These were the first few months of the administra-
tion of President Jimmy Carter, and the nation's capital was
still getting used to the attitude and manner of "the Carter
people," the newcomers from Georgia, the "New South." As
it happens, Moody comes from Carter country: born in
Georgia in 1945, he grew up in Macon, and about sixty-five
miles from Plains, home of the Carter clan. My friend, who
had been a government official, a newspaperman, and later a
corporation executive, had attended one of Dr. Moody's lectures a week earlier, and this was his comment:

"You know, I think Moody has come in response to something that has been lying dormant in this country for quite a
time, just like the Carter people. You feel that he is uncom-
plicated, doesn't want to deliver any kind of 'message' to you
and that he is simply sharing his own puzzling discovery with
you: that it looks very much as if there really is life after
death, or 'life after life,' and that he has seen evidence of it,

can't quite believe it himself, but really thinks he ought to let you in on it.

"And then there's his syntax, you know: Carter-people syntax; it's an easygoing Southernness that goes over awfully well with people who've really had it with Harvard accents and rapid-fire New Yorkers. Moody is folksy, if you like, but sophisticated folksy. With all that, he doesn't really miss a trick: he lets you know that he is a professor of philosophy, but talks about it as if getting into philosophy was like taking a dip in the ol' swimming hole. He is casual about being a physician, as if getting a doctorate in medicine is like picking up a pebble just to see how far you can throw it. And then, with these double-barreled accomplishments, he lets you know that he is just about ready to be a practicing psychiatrist, and he puts it with less emphasis than you and I might discussing crossing the Fourteenth Street Bridge into Virginia during the evening rush hour."

Well, there is something to that kind of Washington-type realism, or cynicism, or awe, depending on how you listen to it. Dr. Moody's credentials are good, but he tells you not to pay too much attention to them. He has told this to audiences all over the country; I heard him, at the American Society for Psychical Research in New York, have read a report on a talk he gave at a Montreal conference, and realize that he is not only a philosopher-physician-psychiatrist, but also has the professional actor's skill of making you feel that every line he speaks has just come, completely unrehearsed, into his mind.

"I know I haven't really proven anything, scientifically," Moody says. "I have brought stories together, of people who have experienced clinical death, and of course the more I heard, the more they sounded like proof of life after death. They aren't, of course, and I am not presenting them as such. You must also keep in mind that I have my own bias: I like to believe that there is life after death, that there's life after life. And that affects my judgment, and it probably, or even certainly, affects my way of collecting these kinds of stories. I'd become known to friends and colleagues as someone who collects this kind of story, and so I probably got more than my share of the experience told to me."

When Moody spoke to the American Society for Psychical Research, his listeners included perhaps a dozen men and women who had spent much of their life studying the possible survival of the human personality after death. But Dr.

Moody disarmed them, too. "I realize that I know very little about psychical research and parapsychology," he told them, "but I am now trying to catch up with all the valuable work that has gone before and that's now going on. As it happened, I just stumbled into this field, and I've been so busy with letters and talks that I've been very neglectful in catching up on these studies."

One of Moody's subjects, Danion Brinkley, told the *Washington Post* (March 27, 1977) that he had been struck by lightning eighteen months earlier, while talking on the telephone. Mr. Brinkley said, "I had to be resuscitated three times between the time my wife found me and they got me to the hospital. I was passing between this reality and that reality. It was excruciating pain because the lightning had fried my nervous system. I had been flung around the room and bounced off the ceiling, floor and wall when it happened."

Brinkley, then 27 years old and living in Aiken, South Carolina, reported: "Then I saw this 'being of light.' It was the purest light I've ever seen. It wasn't a physical being. I went to a place that was blue and gray, calm and peaceful. You simultaneously experienced every emotion you have ever had and your conscious mind puts it into words later."

Dr. Moody is fond of telling the story of one woman in the eighth month of pregnancy, who developed a toxic condition. Entering the hospital, labor was induced, severe bleeding began, and the attending staff was alarmed. Since the woman was herself a nurse, she knew she was in danger, and then lost consciousness.

The next thing she knew, she found herself on a ship sailing on a large body of water. "On the distant shore," she recalls," I could see all my loved ones who had died—my mother, father, sister, and others. I could see their faces just as they were when I knew them on earth." As Moody tells the story, her family members waved to her to come to them, but she refused and said she was "not ready to go."

At the same time—and this is quite typical of this sort of out-of-the-body experience—the nurse could see the hospital staff bent over her unconscious body, lying prone, but she saw them as an onlooker, rather than as the center of the operation. Hovering about her own body, she tried to convey to the doctors that they need not worry, that she wasn't really going to die; but, of course, they couldn't hear her. And then, suddenly, her "outer" body or soul merged with the "unconscious" body on the operating table; she regained consciousness.

Dr. Moody, whether at a small private party or standing on a platform, relates this sort of miracle tale in an almost apologetic manner. You can see that he is going to make an excellent psychiatrist, just as he has obviously been a superb teacher. He tells the story, just as he heard it from the patient herself, or from a colleague, and he tells you in effect, "Of course, it sounds fantastic to you, and it sounds fantastic to me, too; but there it is, for what it's worth!"

There are references to philosophers and religious figures, to Plato, St. Paul, and Emmanuel Kant in Moody's talks and writings. Still, he wears his scholarship lightly: he is a man who is comfortably plump, given to well-worn clothes, totally without the air of a "Life-After-Life Messiah." In this respect, the man's syntax and style is, indeed, reminiscent of "the Carter people," to whom my Washington friend compared him. Raymond Moody, M.D., was formed in the New American Mold and his quietly presented findings fit the New American Mood.

Medical News, the tabloid published by the American Medical Association, asked Dr. Elisabeth Kübler-Ross to review Moody's book. They published her comments under title "Dying—And Living to Talk About It." She noted that she had studied "identical cases," she was "impressed by this cross-verification of material," and found it "an interesting avenue of shedding more light on life-after-death issues— which have gained recent attention due to the increasing number of death-and-dying seminars." Dr. Ross herself has been responsible for the creation of such seminars across the country, directed at doctors, nurses, terminal patients, and the bereaved. She added: "With the increased amount of psychic research and the ever increasing number of books on counseling to dying patients, it is refreshing to see a physician and scientist having the courage of attempting a new avenue in shedding light onto the experience of those who have faced the issue of imminent or close death. Hopefully, such accounts can alleviate some of the fear that so many people have when it comes to the facing of this final crisis."

Dr. Kübler-Ross emphasized the fact that "Man is not only a physical body but has far greater dimensions, which we are just now in the process of comprehending." It may be argued that the other dimensions of Man have been a subject of speculation since the days of ancient philosophers, the theology of monotheistic religions, and most certainly since the beginning of psychical research more than a century ago. But it is certainly a fact that Dr. Moody's special approach has tapped a powerful wellspring of public interest which other, more technical studies, did not reach.

The statistically oriented scholars of modern parapsychology are unlikely, for example, to present the case of a woman who had suffered a heart attack and, in Moody's presentation, found herself first inside a black void and then moving toward a gray mist. As the British weekly, *Psychic News,* summarized this case, the woman was able to see through this mist and recognize "people she had known on earth." She "felt certain she was going through the mist," meeting those who had gone into an existence beyond death before her, and while this gave her "a wonderful, joyous feeling," she could not find words to describe it. This, too, is a common experience; Dr. Moody refers to it as the "ineffable" quality of the brink-of-death experience; for once, Moody yields to academic vernacular: he could have said, quite simply, that many people found it impossible to describe their experience properly, that it was "indescribable." This happens in much of psychical research, in transcendent or mystical religious experience, or even in the happily frequent experience of falling in love!

At any rate, the heart attack victim was unable to find words to describe the joy of meeting her family members in the mist beyond death, but "it wasn't her time to go through the mist." In front of her, a relative who had died several years before, her Uncle Carl, appeared as if to block her path; she remembered him as saying, "Your work on earth has not been completed; go back now."

She reentered her body, rather against her wish, but felt she had no choice. As soon as her disembodied soul was back inside the damaged body, she felt a terrible chest pain and heard her little boy crying, "God, bring my Mommy back to me."

Of course, this is hearsay. Moody admits freely that a case such as this depends on the frail memory of one woman, a person under the stress of severe and frightening pain. The pain itself may well have changed her physical and, to coin a phrase, her psychological metabolism. Odd psychochemical changes are caused be stress and pain. The body has its own peculiar defenses against the unbearable, and one is escape into hallucination.

But when all is said and done, Moody admirably stands his ground. He admits that there are other ways in which to interpret the cases he has collected, but he says in his book that his findings leave him without definitive "conclusions of evidence or proofs." Rather, he has come face to face with "something much less definite—feelings, questions, analogies, puzzling facts to be explained." Dr. Moody has the good sense to be unpretentious to the point of letting his audience in on the way his studies have affected him personally, rather than in a more or less artifically "scientific" way. He finds "something very persuasive about seeing a person describe his experience which cannot easily be conveyed in writing," as these "near-death experiences are very real events to these people, and through my association with them the experiences have become real events to me."

I heard Moody tell members of the American Society for Psychical Research in New York that, together, he and Dr. Kübler-Ross know more once-dead people than anyone else does. If they ever gave a party for all those men and women who have made a round-trip to death, they'd have to rent a large ballroom to accommodate them. In his talks generally, whether because of a natural tendency for give-and-take between speaker and audience or because of the informality of such a setting, Raymond Moody is more inclined that he is in writing to credit his findings with indicating—to say the least—that there is a life after death.

Moody is so persuasive, despite his skillful fence-sitting, because his readers and listeners must find it easy to identify with his experience. To Moody, near-death experiences were a totally new idea when he first came across them; therefore, he relates them with the awe of novelty which a traveler might experience who had never seen the gigantic sculptures on Easter Island, and suddenly came face to face with them. Moody doesn't even, as it were, hum the opening lines from the old George Gershwin tune about love, which asks, "How long has this been going on?" In fact, of course, it has been going on for a very, very long time. And the oldest practitioner in the field, Dr. Robert Crookall—to whom I devote a chapter later in this book—has gathered together hundreds upon hundreds of such cases with magpie compulsion.

Moody's innocence, however, is helpful. If he didn't, in

fact, read Crookall's works, then the patterns he found are indeed very supportive of the British researcher's work. Among the frequent images encountered by Moody is that of the "tunnel" as leading from the in-the-body to the out-of-the-body experience. In his book *More Astral Projection*, (London, 1964), Dr. Crookall wrote that "at the actual formation of the 'double,'" there exists a "blackout" of consciousness which reminded a considerable number of subjects of passing through "a dark tunnel." Moody, in *Life after Life* cites several instances in which people had the feeling of "being pulled very rapidly through a dark space of some kind," and while they used different ways of describing this experience, the "dark tunnel" label is the one which the author emphasizes; others are a cave, a well, a trough, an enclosure, a funnel, a vacuum, a void, a sewer.

Moody cites the case of a patient who reacted violently to a local anesthetic, "just quit breathing" and found himself moving through a "dark black vacuum at super speed," adding, "You could compare it to a tunnel, I guess." Another spoke of "a narrow and very, very dark passageway." Crookall cites various people as referring to "a long tunnel," "a long, dim tunnel," "a pitch-black tunnel," a "narrow, dimly lit passage," and, again, "a dark tunnel."

I find Moody's and Crookall's work mutually supportive. To me, the octogenarian Dr. Crookall is the Senior Researcher of the two, while Moody, who received his doctorate in philosophy in 1969, remains in the self-chosen position of the Junior Researcher. In fact, he confesses with candor typical of the man, that he is "not broadly familiar with the vast literature on paranormal and occult phenomena." This explains his description of the near-death phenomenon as "at once very widespread and very well-hidden." Well, that presumably was Dr. Moody's opinion and limit of knowledge at the time he wrote his first book; but his later volume, *Reflections on Life after Life*, (New York, 1977) showed that his knowledge had considerably widened in the interim.

Moody's second book is based on two and a half more years of research into the near-death phenomenon. It incorporates several hundred cases that came to the author's attention after his interest in the field was publicized. It reconfirms his original findings, but also reports on several new elements in the near-death experience and out-of-the-body experiences, and offers some personal observations on how Moody's own life and thoughts have been affected by his research. He also suggests a methodology of future medical research into these phenomena.

Where Crookall is the collector *par excellence,* Moody's strength is in the area of categorization. To establish the common denominators of the life-after-life experience in anecdotal form, Dr. Moody used the device of a composite case that illustrated some fifteen separate elements that "recur again and again" in such cases. He constructed a theoretical "ideal" or "complete" experience that included all these common elements. Here it is:

A man is dying and, as he reaches the point of greatest physical distress, he hears himself pronounced dead by his doctor. He begins to hear an uncomfortable noise, a loud ringing or buzzing, and at the same time feels himself moving very rapidly through a long dark tunnel. After this, he suddenly finds himself outside of his own physical body, but still in the immediate physical environment, and he sees his own body from a distance, as though he is a spectator. He watches the resuscitation attempt from this unusual vantage point and is in a state of emotional upheaval.

After a while, he collects himself and becomes more accustomed to his odd condition. He notices that he still has a "body," but one of a very different nature and with very different powers from the physical body he has left behind. Soon other things begin to happen. Others come to meet and to help him. He glimpses the spirits of relatives and friends who have already died, and a loving, warm spirit of a kind he has never encountered before—a being of light—appears before him. This being asks him a question, nonverbally, to make him evaluate his life and helps him along by showing him a panoramic, instantaneous playback of the major events of his life. At some point he finds himself approaching some sort of barrier or border, apparently representing the limit between earthly life and the next life. Yet, he finds that he must go back to the earth, that the time for his death has not yet come. At this point he resists, for by now he is taken up with his experiences in the afterlife and does not want to return. He is overwhelmed by intense feelings of joy, love, and peace. Despite his attitude, though, he somehow reunites with his physical body and lives.

Later he tries to tell others, but he has trouble doing so. In the first place, he can find no human words adequate to describe these unearthly episodes. He also finds that others scoff, so he stops telling other people. Still, the experience affects his life profoundly, especially his views about death and its relationship to life.

What, specifically, are the common denominators that Moody found in the 150 cases he studied, and of which he did follow-up work in some fifty cases?

First of all, as we noted before, there is "ineffability," the trouble people have translating their experience, observations, and impressions into words that can relate their facts and feelings in a manner which truly conveys them to others. Many reported that while floating above or in the vicinity of their physical bodies, they actually heard someone say that they were dead. Quite a few reported annoying sounds, such as a buzzing noises, particularly during the beginning of their out-of-body experience. Then, of course, there is the "dark tunnel" feeling, and the actual OBE, which comes to most as a surprise—a remarkably pleasant surprise, at that.

As reported by other researchers, notably Dr. Karlis Osis (see Chapter 6, "What the Dying See"), many deathbed cases speak of encountering others, such as dead relatives who try to make them feel at ease and in some cases seem to form a sort of "welcoming committee." Moody calls "perhaps the most incredible common element" an encounter with "a very bright light," dazzling, and often quite indescribable. As to what the viewer associates with this light seems to depend on his religious upbringing and expectations. Moody writes, "The initial experience of the being of light and his probing, nonverbal questions are the prelude to a moment of startling intensity during which the being presents to the person a panoramic review of his life."

In Dr. Moody's cases, people often came up against a border area, which might be symbolized as a body of water (a symbol as old as the *Epic of Gilgamesh* of ancient Babylon), or simply a "line" that may or may not be crossed. As all those from whom Moody heard did return to life, they turned back or were turned back at this more or less solid frontier. Their return from the experience is often dramatic, and their memory of it is at times in the nature of a lasting nostalgia, although Moody does not actually use that word. Unless they are particularly encouraged to recall the OBE, most of the people are reluctant to talk about their experiences. One reason, of course, is that it is so hard to describe; others have to do with cultural conditioning: who would believe them? Wouldn't they be considered deluded, or at least slightly cracked?

Moody notes that academic and professional questions were raised by his findings. He makes the obvious observation that our lives are influenced by our image of death: "We cannot," he says, "fully understand this life until we catch a glimpse of what lies beyond it." Public response has been positive and widespread. Just because Dr. Moody thought he had stumbled on a phenomenon that hadn't really been examined before, most people who heard or read him could readily identify and share his position.

Professional parapsychologists for the most part ignored Moody because they had been up to their computers in precisely the kind of thing he had just "discovered." Yet, in the *Journal of the American Society for Psychical Research* (July, 1975), Dr. Michael Grosso spoke of Moody's book as "the first sustained attempt to examine cases of persons who have experienced revival from clinical death." Grosso, a member of the Department of Philosophy and Religion at Jersey City State College in New Jersey, also said: "Owing to advances in medical technology it is likely that cases of this type are on the increase. This may then constitute a new class of evidence with bearing on the survival problem, along with other recently stressed types of evidence, such as out-of-the-body experiences, deathbed observations, and cases of the reincarnation type." Dr. Grosso concluded that Moody points toward "an important area of research for parapsychologists who are seeking new avenues of approach to the survival problem," and near-death experiences "demand an explanation which is by no means easily forthcoming."

Another evaluation of Moody's book appeared in *The Humanist* (January-February, 1977), written by Dr. Russell Noyes, Jr., who himself has studied a substantial series of cases of the type reported by Dr. Moody. Entitling his review, "Is There New Evidence for 'Survival After Death'?" Noyes recalls studies going back to the latter part of the nineteenth century, and summarizes some of his own work, notably a study done jointly with R. Kletti, "Depersonalization in the Face of Life-Threatening Danger" (*Psychiatry*, 39, 1976). Noyes and Kletti had found "deviation from normal consciousness that in most instances was quite similar to, though different from, that described by Osis." This is what they had encountered:

"Most persons reported that time slowed and events seemed to occur in slow motion, while thoughts became rapid and unusually vivid. Many described a calm, emotionless state despite accurate perception of danger. A number felt like detached observers of themselves and the events taking place around them. Most felt strange and unreal, and others found the world around them strangely foreign. Both heightened and diminished vision, hearing and bodily sensation were described. Many persons reported that their moments and thoughts seemed to occur automatically or without effort on their part. A rapid review of early memories was occasionally reported."

Noyes asks, pointedly, "Does Dr. Moody present evidence for survival of bodily death?" and answers, "No, he does not. First of all, he presents no confirmation that his subjects were dead, though they were undoubtedly close to it. Indeed, we have no modern-day instances of proven survival of bodily death. Such proof need not be difficult; *rigor mortis* is a well-recognized sign, for example." Noyes puts the material collected by Moody into the religio-physiological category of the mystical experience, for which there is support among "a number of widespread religious and cultural beliefs." These people, he writes, maintain that they "knew" the truth, "because they have been there."

Dr. Noyes feels that, if life ends in "such a state of mystical consciousness, the experience may bring a culmination and fulfillment of his most cherished beliefs." He seems to be willing to let it go at that: "Even if the conviction of a good life after death is only a delusion, it is probably a helpful one—it is better to die or anticipate death in a state of mystical hope than of despair." This is a kindly view, and I interpret it to mean that Dr. Noyes sees Moody's impact as one of religio-mystical Positive Thinking which can do no harm, probably a great deal of good, but isn't Science with a capital 'S'."

Well, Dr. Moody doesn't claim to have approached his subjects with the tools of science, whether these include a laboratory rat or a table of random numbers. What he has obviously done, with his highly personal combination of innocence and perseverance, is walk straight into a mainstream—

an underground stream—of emotional need for a joint effort of science and religion. If Moody's doctorates were in Divinity or Theology, rather than in Philosophy and Medicine, the impact of his material might have been much less.

At a Washington conference at the National Presbyterian Church on March 18, 1977, Moody reiterated that he had "not done a properly systematic scientific investigation," had not furnished "proof of life after death," and wasn't "trying to convince anyone of anything." He added, "I simply find these experiences intrinsically fascinating and worth exploring." But he also conceded that "because people always want to know how I feel, that subjectively—and this is Raymond Moody speaking—I personally accept that there is survival of bodily death."

As it is, I see Moody as a man at a lectern which, for many, has replaced the pulpit. But he knows the link well enough: it was St. Paul, he reminds us, who told the Corinthians that there are "celestial bodies, and bodies terrestrial: but the glory of the celestial is one and the glory of the terrestrial is another."

4. The Pilgrimage of
Dr. Kübler-Ross

It was a cold, rainy day in Baltimore, in the early spring of 1977. Yet, one of the city's largest and most prestigious churches was filled to overflowing. Until then, that sort of thing had happened at Grace United Methodist Church only on Easter Sunday. But on March 20th, men and women crowded the pews to hear an unusual message, from an authoritative but humble source; they were told that we shall live beyond our earthly life.

The speaker who caused this unpredecedented interest was Dr. Elisabeth Kübler-Ross, a Swiss-born psychiatrist who had electrified—or otherwise shocked—millions across the United States with her outspoken and consistent support of the concept that life continues beyond the body's death. After the Baltimore talk, in a deeply moved and highly animated crowd, one woman commented that Dr. Ross showed "the courage of a lion and the vulnerability of a newborn lamb." Another, who felt that the speaker had accepted evidence for reincarnation too easily, nevertheless said: "She is a sorceress who captures the love even of those who disagree with her."

Inured to the television-type slickness of other public figures, the crowd seemed to feel that Dr. Kübler-Ross combined innovative intelligence and scholarship with unstudied ease and a complete absence of pretension. This impression is shared by others who attend Dr. Ross's talks, participate in her seminars, or meet her in person. Listeners feel that she shares her innermost feelings with them; her audiences come away with the feeling that they must protect this tiny, frail-looking woman from critics and other antagonists.

For her Baltimore lecture, Elisabeth Kübler-Ross appeared in a white turtleneck top, with plaid slacks and comfortable shoes. She asked for fresh flowers near her, as she does in all her lectures. She also wanted a lavalier microphone around her neck, so she could roam about and not stand stiffly behind a lectern, rigidly separated from her audience. When people complained that they could not hear her, Kübler-Ross reluctantly climbed behind the church's pulpit—and held her audience spellbound for three hours.

Dr. Ross explained her ease with hundreds of strangers. Her work, her life, her discoveries have made her a neighbor to the emotions of Everyman and Everywoman. She told her listeners that her early life had not permitted any feelings of individuality or sense of personal identity. In order to be totally herself, she had to pick an occupation previously ignored by society. She had not chosen this unpopular path for altruistic reasons, Ross maintained, but "to find myself."

"I was born on a warm summer day in Switzerland after a long and very wanted pregnancy," Dr. Ross recalls in her anthology *Death: The Final Stage of Growth* (Englewood, N.J., 1975). Her parents had a six-year-old son, and wanted a daughter. Instead, Elisabeth, all two pounds of her, was born as the first of triplets. Now she wonders whether this precarious entry into life was the first "instigator" of her later orientation. She had not been expected to live, and neither had her tiny sisters. But their mother's loving determination pulled them all through. Ross feels that maternal care taught her that it takes "one human being who really cares" to make a difference in life.

Kübler-Ross also remembers that when a friend of her father's died, having fallen from a tree, he showed no sign of fear during his dying days; he talked to all his visitors, including little Elisabeth, who recalls her last visit with pleasure. She helped, with all her determination, to bring a good harvest on this man's farm after he died. She writes: "Each time we brought in a load of hay I was convinced that he could see us, and I saw his face shine with pride and joy."

Similarly, when a village doctor's daughter died, "a feeling of solidarity, of common tragedy" was shared by the whole community. But when Elisabeth, only five years old, had pneumonia, she was put into a children's hospital and kept in such strict isolation that she saw her parents only through a glass window, had no privacy, and no toys. She retreated into a dream world of hills and forests, with only friendly animals for company. "If it had not been for my vivid dreams and fantasies," she writes, "I am sure I would not have survived this sterile place."

Although she lived in neutral and peaceful Switzerland, Elisabeth Kübler-Ross, then a teen-ager, experienced World War II with compassion and deep concern. She was aware of "the death toll outside our borders," particularly of "the tortures of Jews" and "the indescribable suffering of those who stood and spoke up." She was keenly aware of concentration camp horrors. During her Baltimore lecture, she spoke of the contrast in a world that has created men like Adolf Hitler and modern-day saints in many parts of the world. "How can you find the courage," she asked her listeners, "to discover the Hitler within yourself?" and she answered: "Only by working through these negative aspects can you become whole and learn to truly love yourself. And we know it is axiomatic that only to the extent we love and accept ourselves, can we love and accept others."

Elisabeth spent her weekends in a Zurich hospital as a volunteer, helping thousands of refugees who had escaped Nazi Germany. Hundreds of them were children. Others were in wheelchairs and on stretchers. When peace came, all these men and women were taken to the roof of the Kantonhospital to hear the bells ring, on and on. One terminally ill woman said, "Now I can let go, now I can die. I wanted so badly to live long enough to see peace on earth come back."

Elisabeth hitchhiked through the devastation of Eastern Europe, seeing horrors left behind by war at first hand, and helping with her medical skills wherever she could. In Poland, she saw the inside of the notorious death camp, Maidanek. Together with a young Jewish girl who had survived concentration camp existence, Elisabeth established a camp in Lucimia, at Poland's Wista river. "It was there," she recalls, "in the midst of poverty, isolation and suffering that I lived more than in all the years before or afterwards."

Her life since then has included study at the medical school of the University of Zurich, a doctorate in medicine, and a residence in psychiatry in the United States. In 1958, Elisabeth Kübler married Dr. Emanuel Robert Ross, professor of pathology and neurology at the Stritch School of Medicine at Loyola University. She is the mother of two teen-aged children, Kenneth and Barbara. Their large framehouse in Flossmoor, south of Chicago, was designed by Frank Lloyd Wright and often serves as a setting for Ross' seminars.

These are the outlines of a busy life, in her profession, as a wife and mother. Underlying Dr. Kübler-Ross' career has been a degree of empathy with the suffering of dying patients that may not actually be rare in physicians, at least at the beginning of their careers, but is certainly unique in sustained and active quality. Dr. Ross apparently resisted the subtle immunology process that seems to affect those who deal day-in and day-out with human death. The magazine *Practical Psychology for the Physician* (February, 1976) introduced an interview with Dr. Ross with the observation that "most physicians have difficulty in dealing with the dying and their families." The magazine quoted Dr. Ross as saying that this attitude develops because doctors "have been trained to prolong life, and have not learned how to handle situations in which recovery is impossible."

Kübler-Ross believes, and has sought to instill this belief in other doctors, that a sensitive and helpful attitude can be "learned" by physicians. Her seminars on the subject are designed to introduce this learning experience into the medical profession. Since the mid-1960's, Dr. Ross has studied the terminally ill specifically, in order to develop her own understanding of their reactions and of how their transition to death might be helped. She found at first that the very study of death and grief was, at least unconsciously, shunted aside, since it is one of the great taboos of our society. As an assistant professor of psychiatry at the University of Chicago, Ross found to her astonishment that clinicians would not admit having terminally ill patients in their care, even in a leukemia ward. The physicians' magazine reported: "So Dr. Kübler-Ross went to the patients themselves. After talking with thousands of them and their families and friends, she began sharing the information she garnered with physicians, nurses, social workers, the clergy, and others."

Two books grew out of these encounters: *Of Death and Dying* (New York, 1969), which summarized the work done in the seminars, and *Questions and Answers on Death and Dying* (New York, 1974), which supplemented the original presentation. Nationwide publicity came to her method when *Life* magazine published an account of her interviews with Susan, a twenty-one-year-old girl who was dying of leukemia. Ross brought Susan to her university class, where the young woman began the conversation by saying, "I know my chances are one in a million; today I only wish to talk about this one chance." She died on January 1, 1970, and this event made a profound change in Dr. Ross, who decided to go out and try to change the attitude of our "death-denying society." After having faced a stone wall, she was surprised by the large audiences who came to hear her talk, and who bombarded her with questions.

Kübler-Ross seemed to have opened a door that had previously been blocked by cultural attitudes and prejudices, by a fearfully shared denial of death. Another major breakthrough into public consciousness came in 1975, when she answered a question from a woman whose child had died shortly before, saying, "It's not a matter of belief or opinion. I know beyond the shadow of a doubt." She has since spoken in almost equally decisive terms of reincarnation, telling interviewers and the Baltimore audience, "Yes, our research has verified it so far."

From an early disbelief in "ghosts" and in after-death existence, generally, Kübler-Ross has worked her way to her current convictions largely based on her own observations and impressions. She said, "Helping patients doesn't mean we help them to die, but that we help them to live until they die." Through this attitude, she added. "People who have learned to live are not afraid to die." One of the strongest points she makes for belief in survival is that when children are dying and are asked whom they would want to be with them, they invariably say "Mommy" or "Daddy," and yet they speak of seeing and talking to someone else who would be meaningful to them, such as Grandmother or Mary or Jesus, depending upon which religious figure would be appropriate to their background; but it is always someone who preceded them into death. If this were simply hallucination, as many would be more comfortable believing, then surely in at least some of the cases, the children would hallucinate a parent who was still living.

Among Ross' findings concerning death are:

1. Everyone knows the time of his or her own death.
2. We usually do not hear when someone very emotionally close to us is clearly telling us that he is going to die, and we miss an irreplaceable opportunity for a close communication with that person.
3. Most people who have died have not wanted to return here.

4. A person who has died once does not fear death anymore.
5. Everyone who dies is met by a loved one who has predeceased him.
6. Dying does not have to be a lonely, isolated experience, but can be deeply shared by others.
7. Dying is probably the high point and most beautiful experience of this life.
8. There are unseen, loving guides within two feet of us at all times so we never have to feel alone.
9. In the next dimension there are different concepts of time.
10. In the next life, no one judges us, but we judge ourselves.

Dr. Ross emphasizes that out of hundreds of reports from all age groups, all social and religious backgrounds, including nonbelievers, only two concepts emerged universally, the only two important reasons for our existence: to be of service to mankind, and to express love. Ever since she has begun to popularize these concepts, Dr. Ross has been forced to change from a concerned physician-psychiatrist and become accustomed to the position of a public figure. Yet, she tries to maintain an essential simplicity and protect her own children from what she calls the "deprivation" of those who grow up in upper-middle-class, white suburbia, isolated from the abrasions of "the real world."

To correct this pattern in her own family, Kübler-Ross arranged for a patient, who was supposed to die in two months, to live with the Ross family in Flossmoor. The patient came into the house with resentment and hostility. The children had to face the presence of a cranky, sick, nasty old man. As it happens, he lived for two and a half more years, and while he overcame his own resentment, the family first developed a liking and finally "a loving" for him, despite the fact that he was "not the least lovable in the commonly accepted sense of the word." According to Ross, it is virtually impossible to help anyone we do not really like. She sees human growth potential in facing and overcoming adversity. In Baltimore, she said: "All your difficulties in life at the moment, may seem like a nightmare; but, looking back on them later, and from a different perspective, you may realize that you would never have grown without them."

Speaking of the various stages of grief, Kübler-Ross feels

that no two people ever go through these stages in the same way. "But," she says, "if you can work completely through the anger and displaced anguish, and have at least one other person accept you—with all your nastiness, without judging you or taking it personally—then you can become stronger and freer, and move forward through the sadness of life." In helping the dying to live, Ross has found that their grief has its equivalent in all forms of pain, grief or loss: "In the loss of a boyfriend, home, job, or even your contact lenses, you go through stages akin to those of the dying."

This underlines the point that Kübler-Ross did not come to her conclusion of the reality of life after death in one fell swoop, as if by a sudden revelation. She may well be right in saying that the ground for it was laid in her childhood experiences, her postwar encounter with human tragedy, and then, further, in her dialogues with the dying. If, so to speak, we partly die with every defeat, separation, or deprivation, then life is a brother of death. Dr. Ross' own pilgrimage toward insight is itself a good illustration.

Over a period of about a dozen years, Dr. Ross moved from a better understanding of the various stages through which a dying patient passes, toward the ultimate personal conclusion that life after death is a reality. She first found that doctors, trained to make people well, are unconsciously disturbed when "one patient after another dies." It is a challenge to their own image as healers, "naturally frustrating, and sometimes humiliating," and it even provokes anger in physicians who receive no emotional support. Eventually, Dr. Ross found, a doctor may become "very blasé" about his patients' deaths or simply "pretend that nobody dies."

Dr. Kübler-Ross feels that medical students need to be taught the "science" of medicine half the time, while the "art" of medicine should take up the other half of their time. The idea is to have doctors become familiar with the situation of the terminally ill, not run away from it, ignore it or deny it. The most difficult task, as she sees it, is for the physician to learn to talk in the patient's own language, which may be affected by numerous cultural and religious factors. Dying patients pass through several stages, including denial of the unavoidability of death, "bargaining" with fate or God for their life, depression over the apparent injustice of their terminal illness, and on to eventual acceptance of inevitable death.

But, with the idea that there is life after death, comes the concept of *Death: The Final Stage of Growth*, the title of Kübler-Ross's anthology (Englewood, N.J., 1975). After looking into earlier studies on Man's immortality, Ross found that her own experiences with patients on their deathbeds closely paralleled those of other psychologists, and of psychical researchers. She told James Crenshaw for his "Interview with Dr. Elisabeth Kübler-Ross" (*Fate*, April 1977) that she found numerous common denominators in the deathbed experiences she witnessed and that were reported to her from all over the world. Among these was the feeling of "a tremendous sense of peace and equanimity," with patients feeling neither pain nor discomfort. Also, patients were aware of their life situation, even during pre-death periods. Ross confirms out-of-the-body experiences: "People are fully aware when they shake off the physical body. At an accident scene they may see their body lying there. In a hospital they may find themselves floating over the operating table, watching everything that goes on and listening to all the conversation."

Confirming Dr. Moody's findings, Dr. Ross states that those who "come back" into their bodies are not afraid to die. Some were urged by entities "on the other side" that they must return to their earthly bodies and existences. She also agrees with Moody that these are not hallucinatory experiences: "They are not psychotic or on drugs or have a high fever that may cause hallucinations. They have a high degree of perception and can, if they revive, describe in magnificent detail the attempts to resuscitate them. One case that Ross told Crenshaw was particularly startling:

"One child did not want to tell her mother how beautiful it was [in her out-of-the-body state] because mothers don't like to hear their children say they like some place better than home. Finally, the child told her father she had met her brother and described in detail how beautiful the meeting was. At the end she said, 'The only thing about it is, I never had a brother.' At this point her father began to cry and told her that she had indeed had a brother who had died three months before she was born."

In another interview, which Kübler-Ross gave to Kenneth L. Woodward for *McCall's* magazine (August, 1976), she told of a woman who for years had suffered from Hodgkin's disease and had several times been near death. Toward the end of their talk, this woman told Ross that, in the intensive care unit of a hospital, "One afternoon a nurse saw that she was dying and rushed out of the room to summon help." As Dr. Ross recites the case, this is what happened:

"Meanwhile, this woman felt herself float out of her body. In fact, she said she could look down and see how pale her face looked. Yet at the same time she felt absolutely wonderful. She had a great sense of peace and relief. The remarkable thing about this experience was that she was able to observe the doctors at work on her body. She heard what they said, which members of the team wanted to give up trying to revive her and which did not. Her recall of details was so acute that she was even able to repeat one of the jokes an attendant had cracked to relieve the tension. She wanted to tell them to relax, that it was okay. But her body showed no vital signs—no respiration, no blood pressure, no brain wave activity. Finally, she was declared dead. Then, more than three hours later, she returned to her body and recovered. She managed to live eighteen months longer with no brain damage."

In the same interview, Dr. Ross told of the case of a young man in his twenties who was thrown out of the car, so that "when the police arrived at the scene, they found him "sprawled in the middle of the street. His right leg was severed, and he showed no vital signs whatever. He was pronounced dead on the way to the hospital." As the man recovered, nevertheless, Dr. Ross was able to discover from him that he had floated out of his body over the accident scene, had observed rescue workers pulling other bodies out of the wrecked car, and even observed his own body, "minus one leg." She added: "You'd think he would have felt miserable, but he reports that he felt peaceful. He had the sense that his whole body was intact, including his missing leg."

Inevitably, Dr. Kübler-Ross' endorsement of near-death experiences as indications of life beyond death have encountered skepticism. Some of her colleagues feel that her continuous, long-lasting contact with the dying has forced her into such a high degree of emotional identification with them that she, per force, had to adopt the life-after-death belief. It is a fact that her personal involvement really began during her earliest premedical studies. She toured postwar Europe when only nineteen years old, saw the after-effects of Nazi concentration camp horrors, and observed the dying in Zurich as they "appeared to be talking to some loved one who had died before them." She told Woodward, "I had long suspected that the death of the body was not the end of life," although she "was never a very religious person."

Kübler-Ross told Crenshaw of a personal experience that may well have had a strong impact on the direction of her research and conclusions. Once, a medium told Dr. Ross that her mother had died; at that time, she, the daughter, had no knowledge of this fact. The news was confirmed later in the day by a message from Switzerland. As her mother had been hospitalized for four years, paralyzed by a stroke, this case becomes an oddity in terms of physical research: did the medium tune in on Dr. Ross' concern for her mother's obviously impending death, and simply hit the time element correctly? Who was this medium? How did it happen that a modern-day psychiatrist went to see a medium, if concern about her mother's possible death did not play a part in prompting this visit?

There is more to this mediumistic communication. When, after hearing the medium convey the message of her mother's death, Dr. Ross asked the "mental question," whether there had been anything she "could have done" for her, a message conveyed by the medium answered, "Yes, you never asked me if I had a headache. It would have been such a relief if somebody had given me something for my headache. And I'm not telling you this to make you feel guilty, but to make you a better physician."

Again, this might have been a telepathic pickup by the medium from Dr. Ross' plagued unconscious (even the reply, that the mother did not want to make her "feel guilty" sounds as if provoked by the daughter's guilty conscience). Her mother had been unable to speak for four years, but could have replied by blinking her eyes, at least during the early stages of the paralysis.

Kübler-Ross' seminars with physicians, nurses and others does mesh with her newly won attitude toward life after death. There can be little doubt that hope for an after-death existence can be supportive to a dying patient. Our secular society, having robbed many of a religious belief in immortality, has left us with nothing to fill this vacuum—nothing, that is, but fear, resentment and a passive surrender to the inevitable. Some people, Ross says, stay angry until the very moment of death.

Must it be that way? Ross told Woodward: "What these

near-death reports tell us about is only the first stage of life after death. I believe there are other stages . . ."

In candor and daring, Dr. Ross at times risks her personal reputation for detachment. This is part of the "newborn lamb" image that turns many of her listeners into allies. Eyebrows were raised at a San Diego seminar on holistic medicine when Ross confessed that she had asked three visiting "spirit creatures" the night before what she should talk about. The visiting spirits had said, "Tell them about us." As Eleanor Links Hoover commented in *Human Behavior* (March 1977), "Saints, let alone sinners, have been burned alive for less." Yet, she found the audience "stunned, electrified, supportive and, significantly, not really surprised."

Without a doubt, the courageous Dr. Kübler-Ross has restated the question, "Do we live after death?" in modern and provocative terms. By doing so from within the medical profession, and from the very center of its significance—that of the dying and their preparation for death—she has done so in a manner that cannot be ignored. The struggle for more and more solid knowledge on this all-important subject must now go on with increasing vigor.

5. From Agnostic to Believer

In 1955, when she first became aware of psychic phenomena, Miss Susy Smith was—as she now recalls,—"a cynical, agnostic newspaper columnist in Salt Lake City." Decades later, she established the Survival Research Foundation in Tucson, Arizona. The Foundation, of which she is president, conducts experiments and aids in collecting scientific evidence for the conscious survival of the human spirit after death and seeks to "establish the results of the research as worthy of public consideration and support." In other words, Susy Smith pioneered and anticipated much of the widespread interest in life after death, and in several of her nearly thirty books, she has dealt with this subject.

To her, survival of death is a reality. How did she arrive at this conclusion? Her experiences and personal evolution differ from those of Drs. Moody and Kübler-Ross, in that Miss Smith started on her search without a background in medicine or other academic specialty, she represents, therefore, much more the average contemporary American who has struggled, argued and wrestled with the enigma of death on a personal basis—and has come up with highly personal conclusions.

Although I had observed Miss Smith's evolution as a writer and colleague over several decades, I have never really asked her quite specifically what turned yesterday's agnostic into today's believer. Even though I served as chairman of the Survival Research Foundation (SRF), and am still on its Board of Trustees, it had never before occurred to me that Susy Smith must, in many ways, be quite representative of millions of men and women today, all puzzled by the clash between our materialist society and our religio-traditional belief in man's immortality.

I therefore prepared a set of questions and asked Susy Smith to "tell all" about her inner transformation. As president of the Foundation, she finds herself on the crossroads of current trends. Aside from the Psychical Research Foundation in Durham, SRF is the only organization specifically designated to study and publicize life-after-death data. At the outset, I asked Miss Smith whether she finds that people today are more receptive to the whole question, or whether the idea of life after death "is still an embarrassing subject to them." I asked, "How do people really feel about it, these days?" She answered:

"I believe people are much more receptive today to the idea of life after death than they have been in many years. When I first became interested in the psychical field in 1955, I could hardly speak of it to anyone. I did not dare mention it to strangers, and there was an 'Oh, Susy, how eccentric can you get' attitude among most of my friends. Today, I am considered by those same friends to have been a leader in a new area of legitimate inquiry.

"Television, and the media in general, have in a large way brought about the acceptance of ESP as a reality, and they are now making it possible to discuss life after death openly. This is true even though most of what they have handed the public in the name of psychic investigation has been erroneous or highly colored with make-believe. I really think Kübler-Ross, and Moody have done more to open the minds of the general public to the reality of life after death, and to the advantages of knowing about it, than anything that has ever come out of parapsychology or the occult philosophies. Because of the authority of their professions, these two doctors have reached the minds of many who would not previously consider discussing the subject.

"The way people as a whole really feel about life after death depends on their previous conditioning and their philosophical state. Fundamentalist Christians are certain that anything they consider 'occult,' which includes the entire parapsychological and metaphysical scene, is 'of the Devil' and should be avoided at all costs. For this reason, efforts to 'rend the veil' are strictly taboo with them. Ordinary Christians are not as likely to become upset about the psychic, but they see no particular reason for trying to prove life after death. To them, it has already been proved by Jesus Christ's resurrection. Today, more and more people are looking into Eastern religions, with their emphasis on an eventual melding with the Eternal One. Their idea of life after death means, primarily, life back on earth in various rebirths.

"Of course, you also have your basic atheist or agnostic, who is not going to accept any thoughts of survival after death until life finally hits him over the head with so many blows that he has to turn to a god of some kind for help. When this finally happens, firm skeptics become some of the best researchers and students in the psychic field. After all, I am one of them!"

Next, I wanted Miss Smith to give her opinion on one of the central problems of life-after-death studies. Much has been written about the scientific difficulty of proving whether a medium is conveying the information obtained from a discarnate entity or is expressing her own ESP capacity. We have examined earlier in this book the views of Drs. Rhine and Osis on the matter. Now I asked Susy Smith, "Can we really prove it? Must we prove it? Or is our knowledge of life after death still a question of 'belief,' rather than of 'scientific evidence' "? She answered:

"In my days as an agnostic I thought that survival really had to be proven scientifically. It seemed to me that only with such proof of life after death could any kind of religion be of value. And yet, during all my research, I was never able to receive anything that could really be considered such scientific proof. I had many psychic experiences of a personal nature that I found totally convincing (some very beautiful, and many quite frightening); but there was no single incident that could prove survival of the human soul to anyone who did not want to believe.

"This is unfortunately true of the vast body of researched and published material. Even the wonderful collection of ghosts who brought evidence, drop-ins at séances who gave their identities, out-of-body experiences in Heaven, etcetera, published in my book *Life is Forever*, does not represent the kind of repeatable evidence required by science. Granted that science is unfair in its demands, the fact remains that no one can say at this point that survival after death has been proved scientifically.

"To me, today, proof is unimportant. I convinced myself; and many readers of my books have been helped by my conclusions; and this is enough for me. I rather doubt that actual proof to suit the skeptic will be found for a long, long time. I have come to the conclusion that each person must reach his own decision by his own efforts. This does not mean that I recommend that anyone attempt to communicate with spirits of the dead. Reading about the experiences of others can be just as encouraging, and certainly less dangerous. In my own search for truth I had so many disquieting experiences that I consistently warn others away from making similar attempts. Since publication of my book *Confessions of a Psychic*, in which were related many unpleasant and dangerous experiences I had with 'bad spirits,' hundreds of letters have been received from readers who were getting into trouble trying something of the same nature. They thanked me for warning them away from it, and perhaps this is the area in which the most good has been done by all my writing and work in the psychic field. If only a few have been saved from possession or even insanity by my words, then my striving all these years has not been in vain.

"I am aware that this is a kind of 'don't do as I do, do as I say' proposition. Everyone should not have to go through what I did, however, in order to prove survival to their own satisfaction. I am a great one for believing, now, that if a supernormal experience occurs naturally and spontaneously, enjoy it! But do not try to force it to happen to you. Fortunately, most people are the type who are willing to read about the experiences and the beliefs of others, and not insist that they become personally involved."

Since I am also quite opposed to psychic dabbling, and find automatic writing particularly risky, I wondered about Miss Smith's own personal breakthrough. Particularly, I was puzzled by the origin of her work, *The Book of James* (New York, 1973). I asked her whether she really felt that the work had come to her from the discarnate spirit of the great philosopher-psychologist William James (1842-1910), who had been a pioneer of psychical research in the U.S. and Great Britain. Also, I wondered, "Could it not have been your own unconscious speaking, freed from personal limitations and expressing itself under the label, so to speak, of another identity?" To this, she replied:

"I've been involved in arguing with concepts all my life. I was one of the many who accepted agnosticism in college. And with no belief in God or in life after death, I was usually uncomfortable, sometimes even miserable. But I could never believe in a God who would allow men to suffer as they do through an earth life, and then just throw them away at death. Neither could I accept the premises about an after-life as propounded by any religion familiar to me.

"It was through automatic writing that I received a phi-losophy about life after death that was reassuring enough to convince me of its reality. For a number of years I attempted to communicate with spirits, first on the Ouija board, then via pencil, and ultimately on the typewriter. My main communi-cant at first was my mother. Eventually she turned me over to a scribe who called himself James and ultimately revealed himself to me as William James.

"I had read very little of William James' writings. When first suspecting that he might be my communicant, I glanced through his *Varieties of Religious Experience* and also his *Empiricism* on a library shelf. Even while reading, it oc-curred to me that it would not be wise to become too famil-iar with his writing style or his beliefs, so they would not influence my reception of the material he was sending me via my typewriter. So I put those books aside and never read James again. The same is true of [Emanuel] Swedenborg [1688-1772]. Yet, Swedenborgian ministers say that what James gave me on the typewriter is much like Swedenborg's philosophy. For this reason I have made it a point to stay away from his books, too.

"In brief, what I was told by my communicants was that consciousness, or the soul, of every human being is in an evo-lutionary state and that one continues to grow and learn and develop spiritually in the dimensions of existence after death. This seemed logical to me. With a rational plan of existence, then, I could accept a God. So with this, I was finally ready for the Christianity I had once scorned.

"The rationalist does not want to build his hopes on some-thing that may turn out to be only a dream, fearing he will make a fool of himself if, when he dies, there is nothing there. Which is rather silly: if nothing is there, he won't know it anyhow. So why not have rosy expectations, and be joyfully surprised when they come true? In my agnostic days, I would not have listened to such reasoning, and there are a great many—particularly in academic circles—who react similarly.

"I have always been thankful that I went to the Parapsy-chology Laboratory at Duke University when I first became interested in the psychical field. There, uninterested in statistical tabulations involving their research projects, I did a great deal of reading in the library. And I was advised by all and sundry to read only 'critical' and 'objective' books. This started me off with a wide knowledge of the historical material in the field. I learned to analyze what I read and experienced, and it kept me from latching onto theories and philosophies without evaluating them carefully. For this reason, all during more than two decades of research and writing, I have always tried to be critical and objective. I questioned the alleged spirit writing that was coming through me and never accepted anything as supernormal without argument. However, when so much came about conditions in the spirit world that was pure Swedenborgian, when I had not read Swedenborg, it seemed to merit at least a certain amount of credence. When it all added up to a philosophy that was acceptable to me as rational, I was finally convinced."

And after that, I wondered, "How did you decide to establish the Survival Research Foundation, and what has it done so far?"

"It was my very agnosticism that caused me to found the Survival Research Foundation. Shortly after I became interested in the psychic, in 1955, it occurred to me that some organization should do scientific research on the survival of the human soul, and parapsychology at that time limited itself to research in extrasensory perception. When I settled in Tucson, in 1971, I set the wheels in motion; and the Survival Research Foundation was finally established on December 31, 1973, as a tax-exempt educational and religious nonprofit organization. We have been publishing a bi-monthly newsletter and have undertaken several research projects. We've had our setbacks, too. And one of them is indicative of the problem that exists in 'proving' survival in some sort of air-tight fashion. We established a Survival Code that might have provided just the sort of proof people are always asking about. But let me give the historical background first.

"The situation was this: In England, psychical researcher and Cambridge professor Dr. Robert Thouless had produced a code with which someone could write a message to be left in a safe file. After this individual's death, the message could be broken by a key phrase given by him through a medium or psychic. If the correct key phrase was received and the code broken, presumably it indicated the survival of his conscious memory. Unfortunately, because the Thouless Code involved mathematics and was deliberately designed to be so complicated that it could not be broken without the specific key phrase known only to the person who devised the message, most people could not comprehend it.

"One who could understand the Thouless Code was Clarissa Mulders, a member of the board of the SRF, a Phi Beta Kappa with the kind of brain good at enigmas, puzzles and codes. With the help of lawyer Frank Tribbe, Vice-President of the SRF, Clarissa took the Thouless Code and arranged it so that it was simple enough for us to use. The SRF Code was presented to the membership, but only a few coded messages were sent in response. One of them was Clarissa Mulder's. And within a year she died!

"Now, I did not expect that it would be easy for Clarissa, presuming her survival, to get her key phrase through to someone still living on earth. But I knew her well enough to be sure that, if she did survive as a conscious entity, she would make every effort to do so, for there was never a human being more eager to prove survival scientifically than she. The first issue of the SRF Newsletter after her death contained a challenge to everyone to try psychically to receive Clarissa's key phrase. It was sent to every medium in the country whose address I could get. It also went to publications interested in the psychic field. But not one of them picked it up! Six months were allotted in which to try to break Clarissa's code; but there were only eight replies. None of them was successful. The message is still on file, and if anyone, even now, receives the mental impression of Clarissa's key phrase—a popular quotation, poem, or song title she might be expected still to remember—please send it to me, care of the author of this book. It was not that I was surprised that Clarissa had not been able to get her message through and break the code. The difficulties of doing that may be insurmountable. What bothered me was that, when the opportunity came to meet a challenge that might really be considered scientific, there was so little response. Today, the main activity of the Survival Research Foundation is centered in the work of our research director, Davis N. Peck of Vienna, Virginia, who is actively involved in attempting to get spirit voice phenomena on magnetic tape. He publishes a newsletter for others of like enterprise."

My next set of questions to Susy Smith were these: "Why, as you believe in life after death, are you critical of reincarnation? Your 'communicator' or 'communicators' are, I think, against it. Do you simply think they know more than you do, or are you intellectually, and on your own, critical of reincarnation? Why? What harm does it do? It seems to help some people." Her answer to these questions follows:

"When I first began reading and researching, I had no preconceived notion about whether or not reincarnation was true. But, from the beginning, my communicants told me that rebirth on earth is a misconception. They explained that all progress after death is in spirit planes of life as *ourselves*, the conscious persons we are now. They said that, because of the reality of thought there, all we have not experienced and learned on earth we will experience and learn at a later date in the spirit spheres, as we grow eventually toward a state of perfection. They insist that the body is important only as we use it on earth to establish our identity as persons. They feel that wishing to reincarnate in numerous bodies places too much emphasis on the physical, instead of the spiritual.

Unfortunately, many people I meet in the psychic field who learn of my unbelief in reincarnation, immediately try to convert me. I used to argue with them, but learned better. So I just tell them, "When we die, we'll learn the truth. Let's not worry about it until then. Let's just try to learn as much as we can and prepare ourselves for something good to come, whatever it is."

My final question to Miss Smith was twofold. First, I wanted to know, "With so much circumstantial evidence available, why do people shy away from believing in or declaring their belief in life after death?" And, ultimately, "Should we not just accept life as it comes to us, and isn't it perhaps presumptuous to try and lift the veil that separates us from our next existence?"

To this, Susy Smith replied, "The only motives I can see now for not believing in life after death are the fear of seeming naïve, or the fear of being disappointed." She also said:

"Although adamant against efforts at spirit communication, I do not think it is presumptuous to try to lift the veil that separates us from our next existence. It is an old cliché but a very good one: If you knew that someday, not too far in the future, you were to move to Borneo for the rest of your life, would you not want to learn something about that country before you went there? Wouldn't you wish to get the proper clothing for the climate you would find there? And to take with you certain objects you might not be able to procure there which you might need? You would not be very wise if you started off with nothing, and no knowledge of the conditions, or of how you must act and live when you get there. As it seems to me, this is the same with the plane, planet, sphere, or dimension of life we will reach after death. The more we know about it, the more we will be aware of how to live now, so that we will be better fitted to be successful there.

"According to my communicants, anything we can learn from here and now will not have to be undergone at some future date. The unfortunate things that occur here and now are really opportunities. It does not matter what happens to us; it is what we learn from it that counts. The more character we have when we die, and the greater our spiritual growth on earth, the more advanced we will be when we find ourselves still living after death. It is gratifying to me to have become convinced that we have opportunities forever to work, and to grow and develop spiritually. For this reason, I no longer fear death. And I thank God that, through my research, I have come to accept and to know Him."

6. "We Need More Courageous Minds . . ."

If you cannot make up your mind whether or not to believe in life after death, don't be alarmed or feel guilty. Some people would much rather live just this one life, and be done with it. To them, the very idea that life will go on and on and on, is quite upsetting. Once, they say, is enough! But, of course, we can't be sure what a life beyond the gate of death would be; it might be so unlike our own present existence that it is neither a repetition, an improvement, or in any other way comparable to the life we live here and now.

If you have such doubts, you are not alone. Not only do millions of questioning and uneasy people face this dilemma from a basis of relative ignorance—even some of the best-informed, deeply involved and academically superior minds teeter on the brink of this decision. Among them is Dr. Gardner Murphy, one of this country's most distinguished psychologists, whose career began with a "quickened flame" of enthusiasm about life-after-death studies, included many sittings with mediums and spirit contacts, but also lingering doubts, sleepless nights of indecision, even severe illness, as he felt caught between belief and disbelief in life after death.

Murphy, whose life spans two generations of American psychic researchers, well might be describing his own quest when he appraised the achievements of psychology's distinguished pioneer, William James (1842-1910). Speaking of James' courage and impact, Murphy wrote that James' permanent place in psychic research derives not only from his views and research but from his daring and energy. In his book *William James on Psychical Research* (compiled with Robert O. Ballou, New York, 1960) he praised the Boston psychologist's "eager insistence upon the definitive nature of

the evidence that at least telepathy exists; his demand that
the instruments of such research, such as spiritualist mediums,
be respected, honored, and studied with an open mind."

Gardner Murphy has continued the tradition begun by
James, never compromising his view that the study of life after death, psychic research and parapsychology, are valid to
our knowledge of man as a whole. As a distinguished figure
in American psychology, he sought to encourage mutual
knowledge and respect between psychologists and parapsychologists and by his own research has shown that a good
parapsychologist also can be a good, even distinguished, psychologist. When the history of American parapsychology is
written, Murphy will rank with Duke University's Dr. J. B.
Rhine as one of its most influential scholars.

Like William James, Murphy's interest in psychic phenomena was awakened within his own family. He was born on
July 8, 1895, in Chillicothe, Ohio. At the age of 16, browsing
in the library of his grandfather George A. King. he came
across Sir William Barrett's *Psychical Research* (1911) which
summarizes the studies made by London's Society for Psychical Research (SPR). Its accounts of mediumistic contacts
with the dead enthralled the young man. In 1957, in the
Journal of Parapsychology, Murphy confesses, "From that
moment the quickened flame never abated."

Both of his parents had been intensely interested in the
question of life after death. Indeed, his father, an Episcopal
rector, had planned to write a book on the subject before
failing health prevented his undertaking the project. Now, the
son took up the task despite his own ill health and great professional commitments.

Murphy found the intellectual atmosphere in Yale University's psychology department "utterly unfavorable" to his bent
for psychic studies. Murphy had selected psychology as the
road to psychic research, to find "the reality of mind or personality as something independent of brain," which is the
basis for any survival of the human soul after death. But he
was impatient with his instructors' haughty attitude toward
such subjects. He asked Professor R. P. Angier whether for a
career in psychic research he would need more than a Ph.D.
in psychology—perhaps even a degree in medicine. Angier
assured him that a doctorate in psychology would be quite
enough.

Murphy's first year of graduate study at Harvard was decisive in many ways. He undertook a small laboratory experiment in telepathy after doing a great amount of reading. At the same time philosophy and anthropology confronted the young man with materialistic concepts that challenged his earlier evangelical convictions. He wrestled with himself in an agony of sincere self-questioning, plagued by severe headaches and chronic insomnia. Finally, quite desperate, he confronted his childhood beliefs during one sleepless night in March, 1917. About two o'clock he put aside his religious faith, although hopeful that psychic research eventually might lead him back to religion.

Continuing his studies at Columbia University in 1919, Murphy perfected a regimen of study in psychic research involving at first two hours and then three hours of daily afternoon reading. This was not, as Murphy recalls, "iron discipline" but self-indulgence: "I loved the material passionately." Soon he was caught between belief and disbelief in the evidence for life after death. As a psychologist he was critical of the notion that thought or personality might exist independent of the nervous system. However, he regarded some of the materials assembled as strong enough to prove man's survival, as "so flint-like that even the erosion of all the sandstone in between would leave them essentially unaffected."

In 1921, Gardner Murphy spent three weeks in London reading unpublished cases recorded by the SPR and talking with British researchers. After his return, still "suspended seesaw-fashion between belief and disbelief in the survival evidence," he made two or three visits to Harvard psychologist, Professor William McDougall in hopes that McDougall might help him get a job with the SPR. Instead McDougall abruptly asked the young man, "Why don't you come here?" There was research money available at Harvard in the Richard Hodgson Fund, named for the secretary of the American Society for Psychical Research (ASPR).

Murphy pondered the offer, talked it over with his mother and decided to combine it with his more orthodox work at Columbia. In a sense, he continue this dual activity throughout his crowded career. From 1922 through 1925 he shuttled between Columbia and Harvard, teaching elementary and abnormal psychology in New York while organizing telepathy experiments and visiting mediums in the Boston area. He had many sittings with famed Boston medium Mrs. Leonore

Piper, whose trance messages had intrigued William James forty years earlier.

During the summer of 1923, Murphy attended the Second International Congress of Psychical Research in Warsaw. This lead to transatlantic telepathy experiments in association with researcher René Warcollier of the Institut Métapsychique in Paris and Admiral Anghelos Tanagras of the Hellenic Society for Psychical Research in Athens. As Murphy put it in his autobiographical notes in the *Journal of Parapsychology*, he "led a double life, keeping a toe-hold on respectable psychology while carrying on the work of a 'quack' as psychologists saw the matter."

In March, 1925, Murphy's career was interrupted when a bout with influenza left such severe after-effects that he remained a semi-invalid for nine years. Eventually he was "rescued by another quack,' " Dr. W.H. Hay, who had developed a radical form of detoxification. Murphy calls this "one of the many occasions in which I found a small oasis of personal reality against the monolithic assurance of respectable and organized science." Also in 1925 Murphy's eyes failed so completely that he was forced to dictate his first book, *Historical Introduction to Modern Psychology*, without ever reading what he had "written." Two years later his sight was restored through unorthodox treatments by Dr. Frank Marlow of Syracuse, New York, who corrected imbalance in the extrenal eye muscles through prisms.

But before this double cure by unorthodox medicine, Murphy had been forced to preserve his strength by abandoning psychic studies for nearly a decade. He had no savings, faced grave health dangers and saw "no margin of safety anywhere." He had to teach full-time at Columbia. In 1926, he married Lois Barclay, who shared his multiple professional interests. While a student at Vassar she had explored the literature of psychic résearch, partly because of the "personal relevance of the material."

Both Murphy's *Historical Introduction* and his *Outline of Abnormal Psychology* appeared in 1929. He and his wife together wrote *Experimental Social Psychology*, which was published in 1931. They devoted the next four years to teaching and writing, and the births of a son and a daughter made them a family. In 1933, Gardner and Lois Murphy studied the famous "cross-correspondences," messages conveyed through several different mediums and purportedly from the spirit of the deceased scholar F. W. H. Myers and some others. When the various messages received through all the different automatists were put together, they formed a coherent mosaic. Murphy recalls that his wife exclaimed, "To think of all this existing and our not knowing it!"

While Murphy was too ill to see anyone in 1928, J.B. Rhine visited their apartment and talked with Lois Murphy for about an hour concerning his plans to accompany Professor William McDougall to the newly founded Duke University in Durham, North Carolina, to set up a parapsychology laboratory. At Duke, Dr. Rhine achieved a widely publicized breakthrough in ESP research by using laboratory experimental methods. Murphy was deeply impressed by Rhine's work, and as soon as his health permitted, journeyed to Durham. The following years brought a good deal of two-way traffic in projects and personnel between Rhine's laboratory and Murphy's group of researchers. Murphy's experiments from 1935 to 1939 showed a number of "flash-in-the-pan effects" in telepathy and clairvoyance, but none were as striking as the original experiments done at Duke. Murphy wrote, "Science does not consist of unexplained flashes in pans, and however much this whetted my appetite, it brought its own frustrations."

In 1941 a group of psychic researchers took control of the badly divided ASPR and elected Murphy a trustee and chairman of its research committee. In 1942, in celebration of the centenary of William James' birth, Murphy taught a summer course in psychic research at Harvard. One of his students, Dr. Gertrude Schmeidler, soon joined him in ASPR research projects, along with Laura Dale, J.L. Woodruff and Montague Ullman. Between 1941 and 1971, Murphy published 41 papers in the *ASPR Journal*; several dealt with telepathy and precognition, while three dealt with survival after death. In 1962 he was elected ASPR president and served through 1971.

From 1940 to 1952 Gardner Murphy was chairman of the psychology department at City College of New York. Then in 1952 he went to Topeka, Kansas, to be director of research for the Menninger Foundation, where he coordinated research in child development, in perceptual learning and cognitive style, and in psychotherapy. During this period he felt that his own experimental contributions were limited, although he was "able to act as big brother to many able investigators." In 1967 he joined the psychology department of George Washington University, Washington, D.C. Failing health limited his activities during the years that followed.

According to a standard textbook, *Theories of Personality* by Calvin S. Hall and Gardner Lindzey, "Few psychologists today are as conversant with the whole domain of scientific psychology as Murphy" who has "earned an outstanding reputation as a brilliant lecturer and inspiring teacher." In recognition of his contributions Gardner Murphy was elected president of the prestigious American Psychological Association in 1944.

Hall and Lindzey devote a chapter in their text to Murphy's "biosocial theory," which sees man as a biological organism that "maintains a reciprocal relationship with its material and social environment." This psychological approach views psychic experiences as part of an individual's social interaction among persons, as in telepathy, or toward events within the environment, as in clairvoyance. Murphy regards man as "an organized field within a larger field, a region of perpetual interaction, a reciprocity of outgoing and incoming energies." He foresees a system of knowledge linking psycho-physiological factors, repeatable experiments and the discovery of underlying principles into a "meaningful whole" that would place paranormal phenomena "in meaningful and intelligible contact with the general laws of psychology."

In his book *The Challenge of Psychical Research* (1961) Murphy presents selected material on spontaneous cases of ESP, as well as experimental data, examples of precognition, psychokinesis and survival after death. He finds that many psychic phenomena are "expressions of unconscious or deep-level dynamic principles reflecting the relation of the person to his physical environment or more commonly to his personal-social environment." He notes that the paranormal usually does not appear to operate when "the normal is doing its work well."

In that book he grapples with the problem that originally sparked his enthusiasm over a half century ago: does man indeed survive physical death? "Where then do I stand?" he writes. "To this the reply is: what happens when an irresistible force strikes an immovable object? To me, the evidence cannot be bypassed, nor on the other hand can conviction be achieved. It is trivial and foolish to ask whether I believe 55-

45 or 45-55. Trained as a psychologist and now is my sixties, I do not actually anticipate finding myself in existence after physical death. If this is the answer that the reader wants, he can have it. But if this means that in a serious philosophical argument I would plead the antisurvival case, the conclusion is erroneous. I linger because I cannot cross the stream. We need far more evidence; we need new perspective; perhaps we need more courageous minds."

These words, written nearly two decades ago, remain part of Gardner Murphy's credo. Today, an octogenarian and retired from the hurly-burly of psychology and research into life after death, Murphy sees no reason to temper these demands.

7. What the Dying See

When Dr. Karlis Osis, who later became Research Director of the American Society for Psychical Research, was a boy of fifteen in Latvia, he had an experience that shaped his future. He was lying in bed, in a hamlet some thirty miles from the capital city, Riga, while his family was much concerned about the severe illness of his aged aunt. He did not see or hear much of their worry and activity, because the aunt was in a room at the other end of the house. He knew that her health was delicate and was told that she might die in a week, or so.

Suddenly, his mind and body seemed flush with an inexplicable joy. Euphoria suffused the boy. His spirits were lifted, his anxiety removed. Something very reassuring seemed to have happened. He could not explain it: the warm, uplifting feeling had not been caused by anything that was said; nothing he had directly experienced could explain this sudden mood, so out of harmony with events in the Osis household at that time.

What had happened? What caused this sudden wave of joyfulness?

As a matter of fact, the old aunt had died.

The only thing we can assume, at this distance in time and place, is this: the aunt had somehow communicated a euphoric mood to her nephew, with the intention of changing his state of mind and to communicate something about her own emotions. We cannot tell whether she was able to convey this positive feeling, presumably by telepathy, before, during or possibly even after her moment of death. It is conceivable that a dying person may, on the brink of death, muster up such a high level of emotion as to break the barrier of our known senses and relay a specific message, if only one of sheer emotion. This might carry over into the very brief moment during which life, as we know it, passes from the body.

But can it also make itself felt after the body is clinically dead?

We have already dealt with some aspects of the concept of clinical death. The Osis experience, and many like them, leave the door open for the possibility that telepathy may operate from the dead to the living. During his moment of euphoria, young Karlis felt that his own room was suddenly filled with light, and he had no feeling that his aunt had passed away; he experienced joy, instead of tears.

With characteristic understatement, Osis has said, "I've done a lot of work trying to determine what that reaching out is, which touched me at that moment, what kind of energy drives it, and how it can be trapped." And, with a shy smile, he adds, "It's ghostlier than ghosts."

The odyssey of Karlis Osis took him from Latvia, where he grew up as a farmer's son, to southern Germany at the end of World War II. He achieved the distinction of earning a psychology degree at the University of Munich with a doctoral thesis on the subject "The Hypothesis of Extrasensory Perception," which dealt with the debate about various theories of what ESP is, and how it works. But when he arrived in the United States shortly afterwards, he was not immediately able to apply his training and talents. Instead, Dr. Osis spent a year working in a lumber mill in Tacoma, Washington. There, his potential subjects for ESP tests were limited— so limited, in fact, that he diverted his attention to the study of extrasensory perception in animals. But even here, the range was narrow: his test subject was a somewhat erratic and unemotional hen.

Dr. Osis' stubborn, aim-oriented persistence to continue in his chosen field of research came to the attention of Dr. J.B. Rhine, who then ran the Parapsychology Laboratory at Duke University. Rhine, a biologist by training, had a long-standing interest in animal ESP. He sent a local scholar to visit Osis at the lumber mill, and the on-the-scene report prompted Rhine to invite the millhand, without his telepathic hen, to join the Duke lab's staff. Osis undertook a variety of experiments at Durham. Among these were several designed to test the clairvoyant or telepathic abilities of animals; others dealt with the long-distance effects of ESP, notably its tendency to fade over distances in space and time.

Dr. Osis began his work with Rhine in 1952. There he laid the foundation for an ambitious, long-range series of experiments into mediumistic contacts with the dead, an intricate system known as the "linkage experiments." These began during his five years with Rhine, continued for another five years, 1957 to 1962, with the Parapsychology Foundation in New York, and later were published in the *Journal of American Society for Psychical Research*, also in New York.

During his years with the Parapsychology Foundation, Osis and I, then the Foundation's administrative secretary, worked under the guidance of the famous medium Eileen J. Garrett, the organization's founder and president. It was during this period that Osis researched and published his now-classic monograph, *Deathbed Observations of Physicians and Nurses* (1961). He sent 10,000 questionnaires to doctors and nurses, received 640 replies, and did extensive followups with telephone calls and correspondence. Osis was a pioneer in examining deathbed experiences, the kind of research that has now been popularized by others, notably Dr. Raymond Moody and Dr. Elisabeth Kübler-Ross. The main difference between their approaches is that Osis seeks to find statistically significant elements in such deathbed experiences, whereas Drs. Moody and Kübler-Ross rely heavily on case histories that are heartwarming and colorful but elude quantitative evaluation. There is something to be said for both approaches: Osis can make claims for statistical validity, while the case histories preserve another valuable element: the human experience, with all its pathos and narrative power.

Osis, during the past decade, has usually had more than one research project on the fire, but an underlying basic theme unifies his efforts. In addition to the deathbed observations and "linkage" of mediums in various parts of the world to receive presumed spirit messages, Dr. Osis has also used funds supplied by the much-publicized last will and testament of the Arizona miner James Kidd to develop controlled tests in out-of-the-body experiences (OBE) and, notably in India, collectively perceived apparitions.

As I said earlier, modern parapsychology now approaches the life-after-death problem from many directions, in an effort to accumulate increasing evidence that points toward the afterlife existence of an element attached to our living bodies, which we might just as well call the human soul. The term "soul" is not respectable in some academic circles. I don't care whether it is or not; it conveys quite well what we are talking about.

Osis is, of course, fully aware of the importance and impact of individual case histories, whether or not they have statistical significance. He cites the case of a Boston physician who returned his patient to life with intensive massage of the heart. When he regained consciousness, the patient asked the doctor, "But why did you bring me back? It was so beautiful." This is a fairly common state of mind. At the most critical moment, during the last two or three hours of life, patients tended to be serene or happy. Another unexpected finding is that the better-educated show more visionary imagery, possibly because they are able to express what they see with more precision and verbal intensity.

In a summary at the end of his monograph on the dying patients whom doctors and nurses observed, Dr. Osis reported that "elated moods were estimated by our respondents to occur in approximately one out of twenty dying patients." He found "exaltation," or "extreme elevation of mood," in 735 cases. Considering that these were people on the very precipice of death, it is remarkable and somehow reassuring that fear was not "a dominant emotion" among the dying. In 884 cases, religious-oriented images that had nothing to do with human figures were dominant. These were along the lines of such traditional New Testament images as Heaven and Hell, but rarely of the Eternal City which the Bible promises to follow Judgment Day. These visions, Osis wrote, included "scenes of indescribable beauty and brilliant colors."

The main part of the study dealt with visions (or, "hallucinations") of people. Visions of 1,370 "hallucinatory persons" were reported. Confirming the findings of earlier psychical researchers, Osis noted that "terminal patients predominantly hallucinate phantoms representing dead persons, who often claim to aid the patient's transition into post-mortem existence." That is exactly what Moody and Kübler-Ross have found. It is also in line with the traditions of Spiritualism, which maintain that a virtual reception committe of discarnate entities stands ready in a manner of disembodied Welcome Wagons to receive and guide those who have just died.

The dying patients who saw relatives or friends, ready to guide them toward life after life, were clear and real, although the patients were at the same time fully aware of the hospital environment in which they found themselves; they weren't asleep, they weren't even in a half-dreaming (hypnagogic) state, and most of them weren't off somewhere, in "a world of their own."

What the report lacked in case histories, it made up in statistics. This, of itself, was quite an accomplishment in a field of research that had until then been restricted to stories of individual incidents that had not been compared with each other, and certainly not on a quantitative basis. In the language of computer calculation, the report stated that the researchers "performed extensive scanning for patterns in the data in relation to the hypothesis of post-mortem survival." The study covered psychological, biological, and cultural background, as well as the actual visions the dying had seen. The deathbed experiences had little relationship to who the people were, or what their cultural orientation was; the report put it this way: "The roots of this type of experience seem to go beyond pronounced personality differences between the sexes; physiological factors such as type of illness; and beyond educational levels and denominational differences." It also said:

"The large majority of our cases came from patients whose mentality was not disturbed by sedatives, other medication or high body temperature. Only a small proportion had diagnosed illnesses which might be hallucinogenic. Most patients were fully conscious, with adequate awareness and responsiveness to the environment. Conditions which have been found to be detrimental to ESP seemed to be detrimental to the phenomena studied here."

"We separated the trends in our data as to those in accordance with the survival hypothesis in distinction from those negative or irrelevant to it, leaving out the ambiguous ones. The trends that related positively to the survival hypothesis occurred predominantly with respect to patients whose mentality was not disturbed with sedatives, who had no diagnosed hallucinogenic pathology and who were fully responsive to the environment."

Looking over the assembled data, Osis found that "persons representing the dead" during the deathbed experiences "were in the majority of cases close relatives of the patient." The nonrelatives, seen by them, "for the most part represented living persons." He added that it would be useful to compare these results with other surveys, "preferably made in a different culture." After Osis joined the staff of the American Society for Psychical Research in 1962, he conducted just such followup surveys, one in the Eastern part of the United States, and the other in India. Reporting on this work in the *ASPR Newsletter* (Winter, 1975), he noted that 1,004 physicians and nurses filled in his questionnaire in the U.S. and 704 in India. Those who reported that "deathbed visions had apparently been seen by their patients" were interviewed in depth.

The resulting 877 interviews were then made the subject of computer evaluations, "comparing the results from both countries and finding out how various factors intertwine." As he had done in his first survey, Osis separated two types of impressions: those that reflected "this-world concerns," and visions consistent with the idea of "another world" of post-mortem existence. Was there, he asked, really a "mountain" that reflected an "interculturally consistent perception of post-mortem existence," or did the dying simply live out "a fantasy conditioned by culture, desires, expectations, inner conflictions, brain disorders?"

In fact, Dr. Osis and his colleague Dr. Erlundur Haraldsson of Reykjavik, Iceland, found many "coherent death-oriented visions" that "ran counter to what the patients expected." For example, they "saw apparitions of deceased friends or relatives who they thought were still living." Osis cited one doctor's report as follows:

"She told me she saw my grandfather beside me and told me to go home at once. I went home at four-thirty (had expected him to pick me up), and was told that he had passed away at four. No one had expected that he would die at the time. This patient had met my grandfather." Osis comments: "Here the apparition appears as an intrusion from the other world—in sharp contrast to the expectations of not only the patient but the doctor, both of whom had believed the grandfather to be very much alive."

Osis asked, "Why did the apparition come?" in many of the cases reported. There were all kinds of "rambling" apparitions, with no apparent purpose. But in the majority of cases, the patient's remarks suggested that the apparition "wanted to take the dying patient away" to another "modus of existence," by "calling, beckoning, demanding." This confirmed Osis' original survey; now, he added, this "afterlife purpose" emerged from the intercultural surveys "like a peak above the clouds and dominates the findings."

Medical factors, wish-fulfillment and religious expectations

were taken into account by Dr. Osis. The "take-away" purpose of apparitions found during the initial U.S. survey came
to 76 percent compared to other purposes; in the second survey, the percentage was 69 percent; and in India, 79 percent.
Also, at death, many of the patients did "light up," showing
serenity or a "peace which passes all understanding," even
while "their relatives are weeping."

After sifting through "literally thousands of computer
print-out pages," Osis came to the tentative conclusion that
"the data give support to the hypothesis of survival after
death." Noting that, in the past, ideas about survival had
come largely from "mediums schooled in the teachings of
Spiritualist churches," or within the context of Western or
Oriental philosophies, Osis concluded that "we can now take
a look through the eyes of the dying themselves and readjust
our research goals and methods in this new light."

This search was aided by an unexpected event: a last will
and testament came to light in Arizona that left some $300,000
for "research or some scientific proof of a soul of the human body which leaves at death." The will had been drafted,
in his own handwriting, by a gold prospector, James Kidd,
who was reported missing on December 29, 1949. He was declared officially dead in 1954, but only ten years later did
bank auditors locate his will and money that had accumulated into a substantial fortune. A court in Phoenix heard a
variety of claims by individuals and organizations who said
that they were best equipped to meet the requirements of the
Kidd will. However, and after a good deal of pulling and
hauling, the money was turned over to the ASPR, which divided it with the Psychical Research Foundation in Durham,
North Carolina.

The Kidd will gave Dr. Osis the opportunity of a lifetime:
he could bring his long-standing personal interest as well as
his scholarly experience to bear on the question, "Do we live
after death?" The research took two and a half years, and the
Society issued what it called its "Progress Report of Research
on the Hypothesis of Post-Mortem Survival" on March 15,
1975. It said that the work had been grouped around the central hypothesis that "some part of the human personality
indeed is capable of operating outside the living body on rare
occasions, and it may continue to exist after the brain process
has ceased and the organism decayed." That's about the
neatest, most succinct way in which the hunt of circumstan-

tial evidence for life after death has ever been put; even a lawyer can appreciate it.

The first part of the report was actually a continuation of Osis's original deathbed study and fulfilled his earlier hope for a comparative study elsewhere. This time, it was a "Transcultural Study of Deathbed Experiences." It set out to find whether what the dying saw could be explained by "this-world sources" or was consistent with an "other-world" explanation. Dr. Osis considered such generally accepted reasons as wish-fulfillment, images that were merely a residue of the day's experiences, or more dramatization of inner conflicts, wishes and desires. Any of these might masquerade as glimpses into the "other-world," but the report found the imagery mainly "consistent with the survival hypothesis," rather than any other assumptions. The report stated specifically:

"For example, the basic characteristic of most apparitions was their having the ostensible purpose of taking the patient away to another modus of existence. After careful analysis, we found that medical factors do not explain the consistencies related to the survival hypothesis. Nor did cultural factors, such as the patient's religion and belief and possible biases of respondents, explain the observations pertinent to the survival hypothesis."

The report noted that most earlier research had been based on "utterances of mediums and represent the possibly biased philosophy of the spiritualist sub-culture of the West. In our research we found ways to avoid the bias of cultural conditioning by evaluating the experiences of dying patients themselves, which are sampled from different cultures and various religious backgrounds. It was very reassuring that the same core phenomena were experienced by patients of such divergent backgrounds as Christian, Jewish, Moslem and Hindu."

The second area of circumstantial evidence for life after death was out-of-the body experiences (OBE). "If there is sufficient evidence that at least a part of the human personality can exist and operate away from the physical body as an OBE projection," the report said, "it gives credence to the idea that such aspects of the personality [soul] could also operate after disintegration of the body after death."

One way in which this type of phenomenon could be tested was the so-called "fly-in" method. People who felt they could leave their bodies were asked to try and do so at a fixed time, when Osis and his fellow researchers had set up "target objects" that these "fliers" might be able to observe while their bodies remained at home. Quite a few people wrote or telephoned the ASPR and made dates for these long-distance visits. Not many of those who claimed to be good OBE subjects actually identified the targets in the ASPR office in New York correctly, and a statistical analysis of the results was not regarded as statistically "significant."

But the ASPR researchers learned a good deal about OBE operations anyhow. With those who did succeed in identifying the far-away targets correctly, it didn't matter whether they were sitting up or lying down, whether they had the feeling of operating in an "astral body" or were disembodied. Those who "saw" the targets best and most clearly had these characteristics in common: they were not conscious throughout the process of leaving their bodies and lost self-awareness only briefly; one minute they were at home, and suddenly they felt they had "landed" on the designated spot in the ASPR laboratory. OBE trips that didn't have these features were usually failures. Also, the subjects usually did not succeed in their task when they reported "separating from the body slowly and with difficulty, and being conscious throughout the exit, or when they experienced "prolonged flying through space" or using a "vehicle" to make their trip. They also failed when they did not land at the prearranged location in the Society's office, or were "unable to find it." Those who felt they were inside their physical body and at the ASPR at the same time, also usually failed. Osis concluded:

"From all such trends, we felt justified in making a preliminary conclusion that the success of out-of-the-body experiments seemed to depend on characteristics typical of the out-of-the-body experience, rather than on general conditions known to be favorable to ESP performance, such as relaxation. This finding seemed to support our hypothesis that the process of information acquisition during OBE states is different from the usual ESP."

This final point is crucial, because it draws a clear line between types of extrasensory perception and the very special OBE, which thus provides circumstantial evidence for life after death. This is a tricky point, because one could argue that a subject might imagine a "fly-in" by his "soul," while in actual fact he or she was only practicing what parapsychologists might regard as purely routine telepathy or clairvoyance.

Another way of answering this criticism was the ASPR laboratory's special method of finding out whether an OBE observation was "truly organized from the point of view in which the projectionist feels his consciousness is located." But how can you organize such an experiment? How does one make sure that the OBE subject isn't just getting an overall glimpse or impression of some object, but views it from a particular angle—just as a human eye inside a human head and inside a human body would see it?

The ASPR used two optical instruments. One it called the Optical Image Device, and the other the Color Wheel. Each of them had a small viewing window, the only opening through which the whole target could be seen. The device was designed to eliminate the use of clairvoyance, which would "presumably be making a perceptual sweep of the whole apparatus and therefore will see the target as it actually is." The OBE person, the report said, "who claims to perceive from a particular point in space should be able to see the target as it appears through the viewing window, at which point it has been transformed by optical devices."

The device, reminiscent of a viewer of photographic slides, forced the OBE subject to "see the stimulus picture distorted by optical illusions." During the experiment, the subject was sitting or lying somewhere else, either in the adjoining laboratory or in a soundproof room at the other end of the building. His task was: project your "other self" to the viewing window of the Optical Image Device; look in; tell us what you see.

Quite a few subjects were presented with this task. But it was intricate, confining and called for the kind of discipline that might easily inhibit OBE performance. The laboratory discovered one star performer, Dr. Alex Tanous. The report, in its cautious way, notes that Tanous gave "encouraging results." As he was available for a full year, Osis could establish a broad base of tests that permitted full evaluation. But even his work, from a strictly quantitative viewpoint, was barely statistically significant. However, statistical significance proved to be "in accordance with the OBE hypothesis." In his book *Beyond Coincidence* (New York, 1976), Tanous describes how it feels to be the subject of an OBE laboratory test. He had earlier experiences in the two major areas that interested Dr. Osis: ghostly images, mists, clouds and other phenomena that people saw on their deathbeds; and the out-of-the-body travel of people who had clinically died on the operating table or as the result of heart attacks, but were resuscitated later.

Tanous himself had been out of his body, and his brother, who died in 1957, had told him of his own deathbed vision. Alex Tanous, while on the staff of a hospital for incurables in Boston, on several occasions "saw a shapeless mist drift away from a person who died." In working with Osis and his research associates, Tanous took part in the "fly-in" experiments that served as an initial test. One of the first of these long-distance OBE's, done by him from Portland, Maine, was monitored in the ASPR's New York laboratory by Ms. Vera Feldman. His task was to "travel" to the lab, describe objects placed on a coffee table, make a drawing of them, and later report his vision over the telephone.

In one of these tests, Tanous said he was puzzled by a division between the objects and colors he had seen. Ms. Feldman told him that his accuracy was amazing, because "the table was divided into two parts." The staff had purposely separated the objects on the table. But what, she asked, had he seen?

"Vera," Tanous answered, "I saw a candle. And something wrapped around it like a ribbon. Also, there was a piece of wood."

"My God!" she said. He had hit it exactly.

In another "fly-in," Tanous saw a basket of fruit, and Ms. Feldman replied "Yes! Yes!! That's what it was!"

Another hit like that was when Tanous saw a knife lying on the table, and there actually was a letter opener. Off the target table, he saw Ms. Feldman drinking a cup of tea at a time when she was with Dr. Osis. And he also observed her bending over the target table while he was on his "fly-in" visit.

Considering that direction of the vision is a key problem in research designed to separate OBE-viewing from clairvoyance or telepathy, it is worth noting that Tanous' usual vision of the target table was a position of hovering above it, in midair. In fact, in order to check the accuracy of his drawings, the ASPR people had to climb on a ladder and look down on the table to match Tanous' perspective.

Once, Tanous and another psychic "met" at target table. While Tanous was projecting himself from Maine, Christine Whiting observed him hovering over the table. Osis recorded this unusual event, saying that "when an experienced psychic was in the projection area," Ms. Whiting "did see the projectionist at the approximate time of the projection." When Tanous had projected himself over "our stimulus display." Osis, said, "he was bent over and floating over the display." Ms. Whiting saw him "bent like a jackknife." She not only got a general impression of Tanous but saw him realistically, saying he had his shirtsleeves rolled up and was wearing corduroy pants. As a matter of fact, he was wearing pants with thin stripes that "looked like corduroy."

Some of the most striking OBE incidents cannot be statistically organized. Once, for example, Osis asked Tanous whether he could locate a former ASPR researcher, Ms. Mary Lou Carlson, who had moved to California. On his first try, Tanous said he was able to see only mountains and water. A house he saw struck him as "strange," not a "regular house," because there was "something odd about it." He wasn't able to tell Dr. Osis more than that. But on a second try he envisioned Ms. Carlson on a houseboat, "puttering around."

He told Osis of this observation the next day. This was a hit: Ms. Carlson was then living on a houseboat off the California coast. Tanous also described the boat and her dress correctly. Skeptics are likely to suggest that all these wonders might be explained by a conspiracy among the participants. Osis might not have known it, but Ms. Carlson and Alex Tanous could have been in contact, by mail or telephone. That's true enough, but this kind of data is not included in the quantitative evaluation which Osis regards as supporting the OBE hypothesis.

In working with the ASPR's Optical Image Device, Tanous had unexpected difficulties. His "body" in the OBE seemed shorter than his physical body, and he had to strain, virtually stand on tiptoes, to look into the narrow opening of the Device. As we have noted before, the Optical Image Device is designed to rule out a free-floating view, including the hovering in midair, which might be attributed to clairvoyance. In order to look into the device, the view must be from directly in front of it. Tanous states: "The window on the front of the optical box is at about eye level for a person of medium height. My projected self, my astral body, as I see it, has hardly any height at all. It's a small ball of light. I couldn't see into the window unless I strained . . ."

The ASPR built a little platform in front of the optical device's window, about two inches deep. This, Tanous says, "was exactly what I needed." From then on, he was able to look into the window and report on what he saw. All this was part of a learning process. Other OBE subjects agree that results improve with experience. As to just how he does it, Tanous simply finds a comfortable position in a quiet room, puts other thoughts out of his mind, and says to himself, "Mind, leave my body now. Go to New York. Enter Dr. Osis' office."

The unexpected is fun, but also frustrating, to the researcher. One day, Tanous felt he was "standing" in front of the optical device in the ASPR laboratory, while he was physically isolated in a steel box. He shouted to the researcher in charge, Ms. Bonnie Perskari, over the intercom, "The light is too bright."

She answered, "No, its not, Alex. The equipment is functioning perfectly."

"I can't see," Tanous replied, "The light is too bright. Something's wrong with the equipment."

Ms. Perskari said that she would make a check. A few moments later, the door of the steel box opened and Bonnie Perskari appeared, smiling. "You were right, Alex," she said, "absolutely right. It was a freak thing—the light illuminating the target was brighter than it should have been."

Tanous laughed, "How could I have known?"

Ms. Perskari replied, "There's only one way. You must have been there. Too bad we won't be able to include this incident in our statistical analysis. Because of the malfunction, we're going to have to scrap the whole session entirely."

Tanous knew when he was doing well, and when he was doing badly. As the Osis report puts it, he "developed introspective criteria by which he was able to identify his most successful tries at OBE projection." These so-called "high confidence trials" during the later parts of the experiment, as Osis puts it, "approached statistical significance." All told, he noted, the experiments showed that Tanous "was in a sense present [OBE] at the apparatus window during high confidence trials, and no indications of his presence during the low confidence trials."

8. Worldwide Search

The worldwide experiment in communication with the dead, which Dr. Karlis Osis originated while he was with the Parapsychology Laboratory, Duke University, applied modern research methods to an age-old problem. The Witch of Endor, in the Old Testament, actually functioned exactly like a spirit medium: an entity spoke through her to King Saul (1 Samuel 28:7-25); she saw it first, described it, and then it spoke directly to Saul. The task which Osis set himself was defined this way: "Experiments using mediums as subjects were aimed at the problem of evidence for survival after death. Intensive explorations were made to find ways in which classical mediumistic phenomena, such as messages about deceased persons, and cross-correspondences, could be cast into modern experimental design."

What specifically, are "cross-correspondences?" When I edited the quarterly magazine *Tomorrow*, Dr. Osis explained this research method in an article, "New Research on Survival after Death" (Spring, 1958) in which he said that "cross-correspondence involves a message from an assumed spirit communicator, a part of which is given through one medium and another part through another medium. The entire message thus becomes intelligible only when the separate parts have been put together." In other words, it's like a puzzle: the spirit entity parcels bits of information out to several mediums; these segments are gathered together by the researcher; the whole forms a coherent unit and therefore, presumably, proves that a central mind originated the information in the first place. It rules out the séance room possibility of telepathy from a sitter to the medium, which is then dramatically bounced back in the form of a "spirit communication."

Osis reported on his work eight years later in a paper, "Linkage Experiments with Mediums," in the *Journal of the*

American Society for Psychical Research (April, 1966). Osis cited Dr. Gardner Murphy's comment, quoted in Chapter 6, a plea for "more courageous minds" in studying life after death. To combine traditional methods with modern experimental design, Osis picked not only cross-correspondence, but two others as well: proxy sitting, and the appointment method. The proxy method is used to put a shield between the medium and a sitter who might have information the medium could pick up telepathically. The appointment method depends on the intelligent cooperation of a deceased person; the experimenter asks, in effect, "Will you, please, provide a message through this particular medium, at this appointed time and place?"

Experimenters can poke holes into all three of these methods. Osis did his best to combine them into an air-tight experimental design. He started by having the appointment medium (MA) contact the spirit (he called it the "Deceased Agent," or DA). At this point, an interested sitter was present. Things owned by the spirit during his or her lifetime, photos and other possessions, were brought along. Once contact was established, a future date with the spirit and other experimental subjects (mediums) was made. A specific day, hour and minute were fixed. The spirit agreed to the use of a code, such as a nickname or a first-and-second-name combination which, as Osis put it, "would summon him."

The first experiment centered around an internationally known biologist. Osis did not provide his name; however, more than a decade after publication of the experiment, we are able to identify him: he was Prof. Walter Kenrick Fisher. According to an obituary in the British magazine *Nature* (January 9, 1954), Fisher had been born in Ossining, New York, on February 1, 1878, and died on November 2, 1953 in California; at the time of his death, he was professor emeritus of zoology at Stanford University, Palo Alto; his whole career had been associated with this university, from which he had graduated in 1901 and received his doctorate in 1906.

Fisher had begun with an interest in botany, but turned to zoology as a result of field trips and biological expeditions. He became a widely known authority on starfish, beginning with his paper "Starfishes of the Hawaiian Islands" (1906). He was a Fellow of the California Academy of Sciences and curator of its collections from 1916 to 1932. In 1917, Dr. Fisher became resident director of the Hopkins Marine Station, a division of Stanford University, with quarters at Pacific Grove. *Nature* described his intensive study of the marine fauna of the Monterey Bay region, where he "built up the reputation of the laboratory as a year-round center of biological and oceanographical investigation," while serving as "an effective teacher, influencing the careers of many students."

Both his location with Stanford University and his retirement activities are significant to the Osis experiment. The British magazine noted that, after his retirement in 1943, Professor Fisher "found time to develop his artistic ability. Having earlier illustrated scientific papers, he now "could take up oil painting" and his "many careful still-lifes and portraits displayed his real talent in this direction."

During the course of the experiment, Fisher's widow acted as appointment medium and what Osis calls a "Living Agent," or LA. Dr. and Mrs. Fisher had been "a closely knit couple," Osis says, "and had cultivated telepathy between each other." Mrs. Fisher recalled that they had lived on an island that had no shops, so "whenever she needed certain groceries she would concentrate on the required items and her husband would arrive home from the mainland with the right things." Mrs. Fisher also said her husband had communicated with her, after his death, through automatic writing, received by her as well as by a friend. Automatic writing gives the impression that one's hand is being guided by a force entirely separate from one's own conscious control, possibly by the spirit of a deceased person.

In order to obtain separate information from the spirit of Dr. Walter K. Fisher, Osis worked through three assistants. One, in Philadelphia, arranged for the cooperation of three mediums. A second assistant in Munich (Dr. Gerda Walther, 1897-1977), arranged sittings with two mediums in Germany and Switzerland. An assistant in New York arranged sittings with five mediums through a sub-assistant in England, and also arranged one directly. In all, thirteen mediums participated. Osis drew up twelve questions which were to be submitted to the various mediums separately. Osis had cleared them with Mrs. Fisher who, through automatic writing, had obtained the apparent approval of her husband's spirit.

In his instructions, Dr. Osis suggested that the mediums, too, use automatic writing as the preferred means of contact, because "the communicator is accustomed" to this method.

But they could use other means, if they preferred. In order to create the right mood or orientation, the mediums were told to concentrate on the code words, "Pink Iris—May Queen" and on a photo of Dr. Fisher. They were to "allow the communicator to express himself freely," and then ask the following twelve questions:

1. Can you describe your home in a sentence or two?
2. What did you use to say to your wife when bringing coffee?
3. Nickname of your wife?
4. When is your wife's birthday?
5. Your own birthday?
6. What was your occupation?
7. On what did you work mainly?
8. What is the first key sentence you gave?
9. On what were you working at the time you had to leave this world?
10. Where did you take your last trip in the earthly life?
11. What upset you once when watching the movie *David Copperfield*?
12. Please give a sentence characteristic of yourself?

While he mailed these questions to his collaborators, Osis himself only knew the answers to the sixth, seventh and eighth questions. As he received reports on the experiments from the various subjects, Osis discovered that his test had been too demanding, was "asking too much," and that its rigidity seemed to "inhibit the flow of imagery." Nevertheless, one subject managed to get the correct year of the widow's birth. Another recorded the same year, but said it was the husband's year of birth; this one also gave the correct months of birth for both Dr. and Mrs. Fisher, but missed the day of the month by two for widow and three for husband. Osis emphasized that Fisher's age "could be inferred from the photograph," but that his wife was twenty years younger, and obviously neither months nor days of birth could be guessed from the picture.

The subjects failed to give countries and localities, although one English subject achieved that Dr. Osis called "an outstanding hit" by stating that the biologist had indeed taught at Stanford University. One near-hit was the statement that Fisher's last work had been the painting of a portrait; in fact, he had been painting a still-life in which the sculpture of a head was featured. Osis concluded: "Although these statements must be considered inconclusive as evidence concerning the source of information, since they occurred mixed with a number of incorrect items, they encouraged us to explore other avenues."

Having found out that the questionnaire method might be too tightly structured for this type of experiment, Osis decided to zero in on specific aspects of a spirit's memory or personality, using "tracer elements." He was encouraged in this method through contact with the wife of a Texas businessman, who was in fact Mrs. Ann Jensen of Dallas (he only calls her "Mrs. A."); she had experienced striking incidents suggestive of contact with a dead friend. Her friend, Ross by name, suffered severe financial losses and committed suicide in October, 1953. After his death, he appeared in Mrs. Jensen's dreams and visions. Once, during a dream conversation, she challenged him to prove his identity, saying, "I just can't believe you are really here."

The Ross entity replied, "So you want me to prove it, I suppose?" His voice had a teasing quality.

"Yes," Mrs. Jensen replied, "give me a sign."

"Would the return of your locket do?"

Ann Jensen recalled that she had left her baby locket several years earlier when she visited Ross' mother. Ross had asked to keep it for good luck, and as far as she knew he carried it in his wallet. Mrs. Jensen mentioned the dream to a friend, whom Osis calls "Mrs. B." A few days later, while visiting in New Orleans, Mrs. Jensen called her home in Dallas and asked her husband whether there had been any mail for her. He said, "You had a letter and I opened it. It had nothing in it except an old-fashioned locket." (Osis confirmed the story with Mrs. Jensen's friend, Mrs. B., who said that Ann had telephoned her one morning and said "Ross was here last night," adding later, "he told me someone had my little locket and it would be sent to me.")

Well, a week or two after the dream conversation—and not at any other time between Ross' death in October, 1953 and March, 1955—the locket arrived. Osis writes, "Of course, the locket did not come from heaven, but from Canada! Ross' widow, who had not been in contact with Mrs. A. for years, suddenly sent it to her." What had prompted her to do so? Osis examines various alternatives. Did Mrs.

Jensen practice precognition? Did she influence Ross' widow by telepathy? He concludes that "on the surface" it looks "as though the motivation behind the incident" was the dead man's intention to assure Mrs. Jensen of his "continuing existence."

Osis decided to exploit what looked like an established channel between two people, linking this world to the next. The first test took place early in 1956. He abandoned the rigid question-and-answer method he had used with Dr. Fisher. Instead, he picked two codes, the number "427" and the word "faint," which the spirit was expected to drop rather casually, into what might be a flowing, rambling discourse. The mediums were told to concentrate on the name Ross at a specific afternoon time on this February 12; they were not to ask questions, to open their minds freely, and to expect to receive "simple, even trivial messages." The communicator, Osis told the mediums, might want to "get through" to them with certain words, perhaps draw something or "try to communicate a three-digit number."

In this case, the assistants in Philadelphia, New York and Munich were enlisted, together with the sub-assistant in England. A total of five subjects-mediums were part of this experiment. Only two of the five recorded a five-digit number, and only one of these got the first digits ("42-") correctly; the others were wrong. Nowhere did the code word "faint" appear. The medium in Switzerland recorded the word "Ane." According to Ann Jensen, Ross used to deliberately misspell her name as "Ane." Osis calls this "a rather improbable coincidence."

Two of the mediums said that Ross had been a member of the Rosicrucian Order. The one in England said so specifically, and the one in Switzerland drew the Rosicrucian symbol of the all-seeing eye. This was quite true: Ross did belong to the Rosicrucians: an unexpected hit, in other words. There were, Osis reports, a number of "apparent allusions to the locket incident," reflecting the locket's suspension from a fine chain while worn as a necklace. The message received in Switzerland was in the form of an automatic drawing of chains in three variations. It also spoke of "something that looked like lace, such as a lace collar on the neck of a woman's dress." Osis points out that this would be a way to communicate the word "neck-lace" in visual form, as one might act it out in a charade.

The British medium also wrote her impression in an "allusion to the necklace, emphasizing lace," saying: "Old-fashioned, with lace, bedspread or something with lace . . . It is a symbol, I think." She also said, "I got jewelry and bits of gold things and material things in my hand." Mrs. Jensen commented on this message as follows: "The lace bedspread the English medium got was, I am sure, a beautiful coverlet that Ross' mother had knit. I also have a number of other things she made—pillowcases, tablecloths, all with lace." As Osis sees it, "lace could have a sentimental meaning of its own" for Ross and Ann Jensen. He noted that the Swiss drawing of a symbolic "neck-lace" and the British statement that lace was a symbol became "much more meaningful" when seen in relation to each other.

At the time of the experiment, Mrs. Jensen received a "message" from Ross that referred to a forthcoming communication, saying that "the letter is on its way" but that there would be "many delays before delivery, say, May first." Osis interpreted this as meaning that "the promised cross-correspondence might be forthcoming in a subsequent session." To corroborate the results of the first experiment, the second would have to produce similar material. Mrs. Jensen told Osis that Ross had suggested using a certain perfume as a tracer, or code. Osis thought this could not really stimulate a medium, and he turned the idea down. But Ann Jensen persisted. On April 6, 1956, she said, "I still think the perfume is a good target. I have a bottle that Ross gave me, called 'Golliwog.'" In the same mail, Osis got a note from the Philadelphia medium, dated April 7, saying she had to interrupt her letter, because "a wave of wonderful perfume suddenly surrounded me." She called it a "spirit perfume" and said this was the first time such a phenomenon had occurred. All perfume bottles in her apartment were tightly closed. (The subject of this experiment has given me permission to identify her: she was Ms. Dorothy Donath, who since then published the book, *Buddhism for the West* (New York).

Well, Osis yielded to this subtle pressure from the other world, and he incorporated the perfume clue into the next experiment, together with the number "574" and the code "fallow-deer," certainly a rare and rather fancy word. The experiments took place on April 9 and 18, with eight mediums participating, of which one was in Iceland, one in England, three in Philadelphia, and one in Texas. One assistant each in Philadelphia and New York also served as mediumistic receivers. At this point, Osis' report adds: "Unknown to us at the time Mrs. A had brought the Texas S [medium] into the experiment. When we heard of this, it seemed a senseless whim because this S had known Ross and had many memories of him which could have masqueraded as 'messages.' However, this was not the case and, as well be seen below, she made a significant contribution."

However, once again, none of the mediums picked up the prearranged codes. Surprise hits came from other, unexpected, directions. The New York medium said Ross' grave was on the "northwest side of a hill," which was true. She also gave the name of his daughter accurately and made "strong allusions" to his son-in-law's hobbies, photography and drawing. The Texas medium received impressions of "lace, handkerchief, cornish or coffin." Meanwhile, the one in Philadelphia, who was used to receiving spirit messages while using a pendulum poised over letters arranged in a circle, received instructions to make a drawing, as follows:

"Take your pencil and draw a line. Draw another line across the end. Half of this line has been intersected very straight in the middle. Take another line, heavier, over the first line. Take another line across the end of the two lines. Now join the bottom. On the left side put a mark like a hinge. Repeat on the right side. Place a rising sun on the side, and a hole in the middle of the sun. Place a long knob at each end. Slow but sure."

The medium did as best she could but did not follow the instructions accurately. She was scared: she thought the drawing would become a coffin, and this symbolic significance upset her. But the drawing did not suggest a coffin to Mrs. Jensen. Instead, it reminded her of an oblong box Ross had owned, with "small compartments in it for rings, studs, cufflinks and watch." It was, in other words, the kind of box in which Ross might have kept the very locket that had triggered the whole experimental series.

As Osis observed in his paper in the *ASPR Journal*, the "Ross personality tried to prove its survival after death," once the allusions in the different experiments "repeat, reinforce or clarify one another." The mediums seemed to have picked up two experiences Mrs. (Jensen) had with the Ross spirit: one, the locket incident; another, being a dream in which of box of orchids turned into Ross' coffin. The references to the necklace-and-locket were, Osis said, "most numerous, occurring prominently in the first experiment, together with oblique references to 'chain,' 'jewelry,' or 'lace' the second syllable of 'necklace.' " He regards these and other coincidences as "too numerous to be easily attributable to chance." On the whole, while he saw these experiments as "not strong enough to carry conviction that communication with the deceased had occurred," they were "too challenging to be ignored."

9. The Case of the
Psychic Kitten

The star performer among after-death subjects in Durham, North Carolina, was named "Spirit," and was a kitten. For decades, the city of Durham has been a center of psychic research; it was here that Dr. J.B. Rhine directed the Parapsychology Laboratory at Duke University and achieved his widely publicized breakthroughs in ESP research. One acorn from this sturdy oak was planted when the Psychical Research Foundation was established, with one of Rhine's associates, Mr. William G. Roll, as project director.

When the money from the Kidd will was distributed, the American Society for Psychical Research in New York shared these funds with Roll's laboratory, which from the start had been designed to explore survival of the human personality after death. Its original benefactor, Mr. Charles Ozanne, had made financial arrangements for PRF to operate independently from Rhine's laboratory, particularly as Dr. Rhine had discontinued survival research to concentrate on various forms of ESP.

As defined in the Foundation's quarterly journal, *Theta*, "continuation of consciousness beyond death" is "the most profound mystery of man's universe." The Foundation studies, and its publication report, "the full spectrum of survival research, including studies of mediumistic communications, reincarnation memories and investigations of hauntings and poltergeists." It also investigates "such altered states of consciousness as out-of-the-body experiences and field consciousness, which may involve survival aspects of the self.

While Osis, in New York, studied such OBE phenomena as "fly-ins" from Maine and other distant places, the Roll group sought to approach the matter from a different direction. It was one thing, he argued, for the person having an OBE to observe other people and objects; it might be even more enlightening if someone else could see or sense the person who was, so to speak, floating around outside his body. But people, it turned out, were subject to suggestion and imagined OBE's when none occurred. While all kinds of methodological fences could be built to keep such errors out, why not eliminate people altogether?

Well, then, what's left? Animals, of course. Might an animal "observe," in a manner not yet understood, a person having an out-of-the-body experience?

What others call the soul, Roll's laboratory calls the "Theta aspects" or TA, which it defines as the "survivable aspects of personality." These, as we know by now, are those parts of our personality that seem able to separate from the body while we are alive, and may therefore be able to survive the body's death as well. Dr. Robert L. Morris reported in *Theta* (Summer, 1974) on OBE studies made with Kidd money, calling his paper "PRF Research on Out-of-Body Experiences, 1973." The most promising subject was Mr. Stuart (Blue) Harary, then a Duke University student majoring in psychology. Blue Harary often experienced OBE states "at night, during sleep." Morris reported that Harary "prepares for them by trying to keep relaxed during the day, avoiding conflicts or other events that would provided distracting thoughts during the session."

Getting ready for his OBE, Harary goes for walks, takes a bath, sometimes meditates, and finally enters the isolated experimental room. He uses what he calls a "cool down" muscle relaxation technique, and once he reaches a certain state of mind and body, Morris said, he sometimes "finds it hard to avoid" having an OBE. The laboratory experimenters have "sent" Harary on various trips, asking him to describe a target or influence a delicate detecting device. The people who monitor the detector are not told just when Harary is supposed to be out of his body. They are half a mile away from Harary's "launch site."

Once the Roll laboratory decided to use animals to detect Harary's arrival in their midst, they set up a miniature zoo. One after another, they used several gerbils, a hamster, two kittens and a snake. The gerbils and the hamster took no notice of Blue Harary's "visits," they went right on chewing the bars of their cages, or sitting around doing nothing.

The kittens did far better, and this brings us to "Spirit." The little kitten was quite a different creature from those detached, impersonal rodents, the gerbils and the hamster. Blue went to visit a litter of newborn kittens at a neighbor's one day, and as he sat among them, one of the baby cats "Spirit," moved up to him. Morris reports, "a second then went up to the first kitten "and played with it." Harary picked Kitten No. 1, "because it showed an affinity for him" and took the second one "as company for the first." As it turned up, Kitten No. 1 later responded to Harary's OBE, but Kitten No. 2, named "Soul," did not show an obvious response.

Now, let me give you an idea of how these experiments with small animals work. The basic problem is to find a way of quantifying the results. To do this, the animals' movements are recorded, to see whether they are relaxed or restless, prefer one part of a cage of container to another. Morris reports:

"The first study used a three-foot-deep 'open field' container. The floor, which measured 30 by 80 inches, was divided into 24 numbered, ten-inch squares. Each kitten was run individually and its activity observed during two preliminary periods followed by two minute experimental periods, one during an OBE and one during a time when Blue was aroused and talking with the researchers. During the first session, both kittens were very active: They crossed a large number of squares, vocalized (meowed) frequently and attempted to get out. The second session produced similar results, except that one kitten ["Spirit"] became strikingly quiet during an experimental period, crossing only one square, not vocalizing or attempting to escape and behaving in a very calm manner. This turned out to be an OBE period. We then focused attention only on that kitten and ran a formal experimental series consisting of four sessions, each containing two OBE and two non-OBE observation periods. The observers did not know which was which."

The result was really quite striking. When Harary was not having an OBE or "visiting" the kitten, "Spirit" was quite restless and moved around a good deal. But when Blue Harary came to "visit," the baby cat seemed to see or sense his presence, found it agreeably soothing, and neither moved around as much, nor meowed restlessly. Morris found that during these visits "Spirit" "became very quiet," and the difference in movement and sounds ("for both squares and vocalizations") was statistically meaningful: in other words, the difference between the two periods was great enough to show a quantitative significance.

When Harary was not having an OBE, "Spirit" meowed thirty-seven times; but during the OBE period, the animal didn't even meow once! When there was no OBE, the cat kept trying to get out of its container; but when Harary willed himself to make an OBE "visit," the cat "did not show this behavior at all." Morris summarizes: "It was as though the cat detected the experience and responded by being calm and contented where it was."

When a snake was used for a similar experiment involving Harary's OBE, it first started to strike and gnaw at the glass front of its cage; it didn't, as a rule, do this sort of thing. But later, both during OBE periods and at other times, the snake didn't do any striking or gnawing. "Thus, the snake was either not capable of detection," Morris concluded, "or, if it was, its response rapidly habituated, making it not very useful." Which amounts to the speculation that to the kitten an OBE intrusion is a major event, soothing when it involves a friend, whereas this snake didn't respond much, one way or another.

With the psychic kitten emerging as a star performer, while the rodents and the snake remained indifferent—what, after all, was the reaction of *people?*

The researchers did not find much difference between people's responses, whether right or wrong. Expectations seemed to ruin responses. Or, as Morris puts it, "most humans become self-conscious when concentrating on detection, try too hard, and so on." Anyway, results did not show any statistical significance. But people who were operating equipment, and did not consider themselves participants in the experiments, had occasional "spontaneous detection experiences." These were rare, but, Harary recalls, "always correct."

Blue Harary was also asked to try and influence delicate detection devices during his OBE's. Among them were machines designed to measure electromagnetic field strength and electromagnetic permeability of the surrounding air, thermocouples and photo-multiplier tubes. Various monitoring devices were used, including an oscilloscope. Some small, unexplained changes took places, but these could not be convincingly linked to Harary's OBE's. Morris assumes that

Harary's disembodied self "may increase already existing physical activity in the area he visits, but does not appear to initiate such activity in the frequency ranges so far examined."

Like Alex Tanous, Ingo Swann and others, Harary also engaged in what by now are fairly standard OBE tests: that is, he was supposed to "visit" and "read" specific targets. At one point, the other experimenters placed colored alphabet letters on a wall in a room Harary was supposed to "visit" while having an OBE. On the whole, the results were not statistically significant, although in some instances his descriptions were quite accurate.

A few times, he was supposed to pick out people. The idea was to give him three spots he might decide to visit, but in only one spot would he find somebody waiting for him. He did fine the first night, with two different out-of-the-body trips. After that, he seemed to decline, and overall results weren't significant.

As happens too often in well-planned experiments, unexpected side effects are fascinating, whether or not they can be quantified. For example, when Blue had his first cat-finding OBE, he thought both kittens would be in their container. He left the detection laboratory and went to the "launching site," a psychophysiological laboratory, assuming both cats would be used. But while Blue was gone, Morris found he could not keep track of the movements and meows of two kittens, so he lifted "Soul" out of the box. When Harary went into his out-of-the-body state and made his soul-visit to the cat container, he was puzzled to find only one of the kittens, and thought he had made a mistake. On the contrary, he'd made a perfect hit.

In a preceding chapter, we saw that Tanous had complained the lights in one experiment had been accidentally turned up, too bright for him to practice his OBE effectively. Morris reports that Harary was able to tell whether detection room lights were on and off: "He reported clear vision and brightness when they were off, and he reported difficult in seeing when, in fact, the lights were on." As in Tanous' case, excessive brightness was a hindrance, rather than a help.

Harary and Roll reported on their OBE work at the Southern Regional Parapsychological Association in January, 1976, telling about one experiment in which Blue was supposed to "visit" five unknown three-dimensional targets. These were sufficiently different in nature, size and shape to make them clearly distinguishable from each other; they were: a bottle, two frisbees, an oboe, and a black rectangular oboe case. Harary didn't know what they were beforehand, nor was he told how many objects he might expect to be used as targets for his OBE.

Harary had a feeling of success when he had his OBE, and he reported, "Round, flat object like a plate . . maybe something black and square . . . saw two things; both might have been the same thing . . . something tall standing in middle . . . something round . . . maybe a frisbee on top . . . maybe saw a bottle." This was obviously a successful experiment, the round object clearly the frisbee, and even the frisbee called by its name! The reference to two items of a kind was also striking. On another occasion, however, when Harary felt it was "not a clear night" in his OBE, he didn't hit a single target right.

In a totally different experiment, Harary was supposed to send his disembodied self to visit someone who was playing tape-recorded music, including a vocal piece Harary had no reason to expect. However, he did, as *Theta* reported (Summer, 1976) "accurately describe the music that was playing during this OBE." The same report stated that Harary was originally supposed to zero in on "an abstract magenta and orange target" provided by a light-display board, although this target had at the last moment been substituted for a single-color letter of the alphabet. Again, he did well; he "described and drew a very close approximation of this target, including its colors, before the target was known."

Back of the Harary experiences, and those recorded outside Roll's laboratory by Dr. Osis in New York, Dr. Charles Tart of the University of California at Davis, and other present-day U.S. researchers, lies a vast literature of a more anecdotal and less rigidly scientific nature. That it is, for the most part, in a religio-occult tradition, highly subjective and emotionally colored, shouldn't discourage us from seeing it as tributaries that have contributed to today's unified stream of research into possible post-mortem survival by means of out of the body experiences.

Modern parapsychologists prefer the OBE label to older and more esoteric-sounding names, such as "astral travel" or "traveling clairvoyance." But the phenomena are essentially identical.

There is a pervasive scientific attitude that, if you can't capture or repeat something in a controlled laboratory setting, is doesn't happen. That's okay, as far as it goes. But how, for example, do you "replicate in an experimental setting" the act of falling in love? Yet, as most of us can testify, it's real, all right! And if someone claims that, at a time of physical or emotional stress, he felt something like his soul seeming to escape from his body and go a-traveling, he needn't be a liar, needn't be deluded, and may very well be telling the truth. But then, again, he may also be telling a tall tale.

The trouble is that we all share a childhood yearning of being invisible, of traveling where our imagination wishes us to travel. And in dreams, primitive man has long thought that he is, indeed, visiting faraway places, including the world of the dead. In addition to the terms mentioned above, the word "bi-location," being in two places at the same time, has long been part of a certain type of fiction, as well as of the literature of psychopathology.

All this is said, because the Harary experiments didn't yield a big batch of significant data. In fact, it all comes down to what Dr. Morris, with mixed modesty and exasperation, summed up this way: "Our best results were with the kitten. They support anecdotal stories that animals, particularly family pets, respond to their masters in the out-of-body state. The studies involving humans and physical detectors are indefinite and need refinement and repetition."

Blue Harary's personal views of what actually happens during a so-called out-of-the-body experience suggest that we have, perhaps, gone too far in generalizing and categorizing this experience. He challenges the assumption that, during the OBE, there really is something—the soul, an essence of personality—that leaves the body, floats around and actually separates itself. It is true, he says, that "it does feel as if you were separate from your physical body, but I think we have gone too far in accepting something we do not actually know, do not really understand, and can only describe in possibly misleading subjective terms."

Harary adds that "the feeling that you are, in fact, separate from your body is very strong." But, he asks, is it real? You might feel that you are the cabinet across the room, but this does not necessarily mean that you are. So, he insists, "we must keep in mind that all this separation we talk about, has not really been established—anymore than we have established that mind and body were put together, in the first place." I never will say, he adds, "unless something very, very drastically convincing makes me change my mind," that I have moved "outside my body," only that "it certainly feels that way."

A thorough and thoughtful appraisal of the whole field of this inquiry has been published by William G. Roll, project director of the Psychical Research Foundation, under the title "Theta Project: A study of the Process of Dying, Death, and Possible Continuation of Consciousness after Death," which appeared in *Theta* (Summer, 1976). He reviewed the research done, thus far, "in the exploration of the living personality or consciousness as it appears to extend beyond the physical organism." Now, he said, it is time to "apply the knowledge gained from these studies to an exploration of dying and death." If death is actually what we have come to call an "altered state of consciousness," it might well continue after "the brain has then ceased functioning."

Roll explores the alternatives and hypotheses that have been put forward in this search. Perhaps, he quotes one authority, the living form a new unit after death; when one member of a group dies, "there may be a natural flow of information with the survivors." He recalls that "families and other closely knit groups" were most successful in post-mortem contacts through mediums. Collaboration between scientifically trained people who are expected to die soon (the elderly, or cancer patients) are favored to work together "before death, during death, and after death."

William Roll places a good deal of emphasis on preparation for the "after-death environment," including study of such works as *The Tibetan Book of the Death* and the current inspirational-educational volume, *A Course in Miracles*. Getting ready for death, and for after-death communication with the living is, in Roll's view, a traditional as well as currently desirable educational process. Codes between the dead and the living should be utilized, and word association tests employed to establish identity.

Roll does not see the investigator in this field as a totally detached, cold and purely analytical factor. Instead, he feels the investigator, at his best, "interacts with or is part of the situation he explores," and his personal relation to the subjects, and his purpose in undertaking the research, together with his general state of consciousness at the time, may affect the outcome of his research.

I've had a feeling right along that most researchers in the survival of the human personality after death have their own highly charged involvement with the question—much as many physicians select a medical career because it gives them a feeling of omnipotence in dealing with patients, and their profession acts as a partly imaginary shield against illness and early death.

These are weighty and profound thoughts. The kitten that sensed the out-of-the-body experience of his friend Blue Harary may yet go down in the history of human immortality. I, for one, am willing to contribute to an appropriate statue of "Spirit," in the little cat's memory as a scientific hero.

10. And What About Animals?

If people live after death—how about animals? And, specifically, what about beloved animal friends—pet dogs and cats? I know one woman who, quite frankly, doesn't very much look forward to seeing her departed husband in a world beyond death, but anticipates a reunion with her pet cats with real pleasure. Certainly, by rights, animals should survive death, just as people do (if they do!). The numerous animal-lovers among us would hardly consider an afterlife heavenly if it did not include the company of a beloved pet.

The experiments with "Spirit," the psychic kitten, and Dr. Rhine's blueprint for future survival experiments with animals, provide a framework for scientific research in this field. But let us, in this chapter, put aside the academic forms of "proof" and examine some purely personal stories of apparent evidence for animal survival after death.

Personal evidence is abundant. Ghosts of animals have been seen almost as often as ghosts of humans. "For fourteen years I had a dog named Rover," G. Reeves of Brooklyn wrote to *The Star* (January 7, 1973). A week after he died I saw him appearing at the glass door. I watched as he walked through the closed door and lay down on the rug." Reeves was glad for the corroboration that his mother also saw Rover at the same time, although neither of them ever saw him again.

In *More ESP For the Millions* (Los Angeles, 1969), Susy Smith tells of Sam, a Siamese cat who had "the cutest big grin" according to his owner, Mrs. James Merrick of Miami, Florida. Sam was unusually friendly and loved attention, so it is probably natural that he stayed around home ever since his death at the age of seven in July, 1965. The first time Jane Merrick saw the cat's ghost was one evening about two weeks after he died. She turned while preparing dinner and

Sam was back of her. She mechanically stepped aside to keep from treading on him, just as she had done so many times in the past. Then, of course, she remembered that he had "gone away." At that moment he disappeared, "Just like that!" said Jane, snapping her fingers.

Mrs. Merrick said that the longest and most realistic vision she had of Sam occurred several weeks later when she was standing at the sink in the kitchen and happened to turn her head. "I saw him come around the corner of a chair in the living room and jump up onto it," she said. "I could see only his form, his face was not clear, but it was Sam's tiger walk exactly. I could identify his color and his walk perfectly. His face was rather misty, but it was definitely Sam. I just stood there amazed, not knowing what to think of it, and then he disappeared."

Miss Smith reported on another cat ghost from Miami, as seen by Chérie Hughes. Chérie said: "When I was a child I had a lovely fluffy silver Persian cat named Mimi. She lived to the ripe old cat age of about nineteen. She used to love to run up and down steps, and got lots of exercise that way. She's still at it! Very frequently now she comes racing through the house and up or down stairs. Sometimes I will see her. Sometimes my son picks her up with his eyes as she flashes by. John will say, 'Oops, there goes the cat again!'" Their dog, a silver-gray mini-poodle named Panache, also sees Mimi. He bristles a little, but "he doesn't say much, just a little growl."

These stories suggest that animals who have died tend to live at least for a time where they previously lived and follow their former routines. Nina Epton's book *Cat Manners and Mysteries* gives many instances of cats who have returned from the dead and been observed by their owners in familiar surroundings. As quoted in *Modern People* (June 6, 1976), a cat belonging to Miss D. Cullen, who was put to sleep because of illness, reappeared on several occasions.

"At dawn, she came into my room and I saw her clearly. I heard her for many nights jumping on her chair, and getting a drink of water." Miss Cullen also felt her pet place her chin on her arm in a customary manner.

When Mrs. L. Justice of Loves Park, Illinois, was an "unloved foster child," she says her life was made joyous for a time by Jipsey, a small nondescript, long-haired dog, who belonged to a neighbor. She says in *The Star* that they romped together all the time. One day Jipsey was there when the child went out to play, dancing about and waggling her tail as usual, but, says Mrs. Justice, "I couldn't catch her. She would follow me or run ahead of me but I couldn't pick her up." She mentioned this at the dinner table that night, but only encountered stares of unbelief. Then she was told that she could not have played with Jipsey that day because the little dog had been killed by a car the day before. Jipsey, the child was told, had been buried in the neighbor's yard, with a rosebush over her grave. She writes, "I rushed to the grave, and there stood Jipsey, wagging her tail joyously. When I knelt to pet her, she slipped away and was gone. I never saw her again."

Animals are heard after their deaths, apparently as often as they are seen. Bill Schul in *The Psychic Power of Animals* (New York, 1976), tells of his dachshund, Phagen, who announced his own death by barking. Schul says that late one night he was awakened from a deep sleep by Phagen's persistent barking. After a few minutes, when the barking continued sharp and quite insistent, Schul pulled on a robe and slippers and made his way to Phagen's pen. The dog was not outside. When Bill looked inside the doghouse with his flashlight, there Phagen's body lay. He had obviously been dead for several hours, for he was frozen stiff.

Phagen barked for the next two nights at exactly the same hour. Both nights, Bill went outside. The first night he saw nothing but an empty pen and house. The second night, as he approached the pen in the semi-darkness of a waning moon, he saw his pet in the shadows, waiting. As he drew closer, he saw the animal wag his tail, but as he reached toward him, he was gone. Schul writes: "He never barked again. Was he just telling us farewell? Had he come back that night for a final goodbye? Was I stumbling out of my dreams and passing headlong into hallucinations? One might ponder this question except that my neighbor, who was not aware that our dog had died, asked me the morning following my final experience if something was wrong with Phagen as he had barked so much the night before."

Noelle Fojut of Tucson, Arizona, saw her Siamese cat a month after she died in 1975. It was a windy night and Mrs. Fojut looked out of her window and saw the recently deceased Mummy Cat in the back yard. Because it was such a dark sealpoint Siamese, it could not be confused with her other two cats. Nonetheless, she checked and found the two contentedly sleeping in other areas of the yard.

Noelle also has had the experience of "feeling" a deceased animal. As she entered the home of a friend, she was almost knocked over by a small dog running between her legs, rushing to get outside. She remembered only later that this little fellow had died several months before.

Some animals who have died manage to reveal themselves later in a variety of different ways. Ronnie, a twelve-year-old cocker spaniel, was nearly blind and deaf when he had to undergo an operation. Elaine V. Worrel in "Psychic Contact with Animals" *Exploring the Unknown* (October 1969), says that on July 4, 1960, she sat in the kitchen near the phone, awaiting the vet's call to tell her whether her pet had survived an operation. "A few minutes after nine I heard the tinkle of Ronnie's dogtags and the tapping of his claws coming slowly across the porch to the front door. I arose and held the screen door open before it dawned on me that Ronnie was at the veterinary's. I started to cry then, still holding the door open." She knew her old friend had passed on. Then she heard the tinkle of his dogtags coming near her knee, and her tears stopped. He was, she felt, letting her know he had come home.

Her next door neighbor, Janet Mounce, came in that Friday after work for a cup of coffee. "Oh, did Ronnie get in the house all right Tuesday morning, Elaine?" she asked. "I was late for work or I would have put him in the car and brought him back as I usually do when he wanders up the street. Poor old fellow, he was halfway up the block, coming home. I said a prayer he'd make it before the school bus came."

"You didn't see him, Janet," Mrs. Worrel said.

Her Texas temper showed a little. "Are you trying to tell me I don't know Ronnie when I see him? I've lived next door to him for five years."

Even when told that the dog had died that morning, Janet refused to believe she had not seen him in the flesh until the children came in and told her the same thing.

There are even stories of how deceased pets have saved the lives of those they loved. A good one comes from the *National Enquirer* (January 7, 1973), written by Nicole Lieberman. "Norma and Tom Kresgal owe their lives to the ghostly bark of a long-dead pet collie," she wrote. Corky, Mrs.

Kresgal's devoted companion for about seven years, was noted for the strange croaking sound he made when he tried to bark. This was caused by a permanent injury to his voice box, once, when he was shot. He died in 1953. Two years later the Kresgals moved to New York City where they lived in an upstairs apartment of a two-family house in Queens.

"We were living there only a few months," says Norma, "when I was suddenly awakened one night by a strange sound. It was Corky's hoarse bark. I thought I was dreaming and was about to go back to sleep when I heard him again—loud and clear."

She got up to see whether another dog was in the house, with a strange bark like Corky's. But when she opened the door of her bedroom, great clouds of smoke drove her back. She awoke her husband and their landlord, and they escaped before the house became engulfed by flames. She cried tears of gratitude, "thanking God with all my heart for letting my Corky come back to me long enough to arouse me—before it was too late."

A dead dog's barking scared off a burglar in the apartment complex of Mrs. Lowanda Cady of Wichita, Kansas. One night Jock barked and woke up his mistress, who heard hurried footsteps in the rooms below, accompanied by the barking Jock. When Mrs. Cady investigated, she discovered that the intruder had been helping himself to the contents of her refrigerator. She turned to thank her dog, and then suddenly remembered that he had died three months before. One can't help but wonder at the reaction of the burglar, with an invisible dog barking at his heels. Or perhaps he saw Jock as well as heard him.

Other animals besides the dogs and cats we have mentioned have been seen, not only as ghosts but also by visitors to "spirit realms." Harriet M. Shelton, author of *Abraham Lincoln Returns* (New York, 1957), saw a lion while she was having an out-of-body experience and traveling in what she referred to as the "astral plane." She asked the "guide" who was conducting her tour if she should be afraid of it. He replied, "What do you think?" Just then the lion came up and rubbed its head against her leg as if it were a big, friendly cat.

Interestingly enough, a pet dog in the physical realm entered the room at that moment and flopped down on the floor at Mrs. Shelton's feet. Apparently his vision took in the area in which Mrs. Shelton was traveling, for he jumped up and ran yipping, out of the room.

A friend of Bill Schul's reported seeing a pet while having an out-of-body experience. He said, "On one occasion I clearly saw Ben, my old collie who had died several months before. He was beside himself to see me, wagging his tail and jumping up against me. I petted him, talked to him, and never doubted the reality of the experience."

Strikingly similar is the incident reported by Susy Smith in *Confessions of a Psychic* (New York, 1971). which involved her miniature dachshund, Junior, who had died six months earlier. Miss Smith was in a hotel in London in the fall of 1973. She awoke early and drifted into a light doze. "Suddenly I was with Junior," she writes. "My dog saw me, perked up his ears, then leaped on me with his usual affection. Holding him in my arms as he joyously licked my face and expressed his happiness at seeing me, I just as delightedly hugged and petted his squirming body. And asked myself what the *hell* was going on.

" 'This is *not* a dream,' I declared emphatically, and it wasn't. It was in no possible way dreamlike."

Miss Smith concluded, even during the happy reunion with her pet, that she was having an out-of-body experience, within another dimension of space.

Mrs. Shelton's adventure with the lion makes us realize that other animals can make themselves known after death. Birds have been seen and heard singing and so have other pets. The Paris medium Hélène Bouvier, as reported in Simone Saint-Clair's *Une Voyante Témoigne* (Paris, 1966), once saw a horse. "The horse was very happy, placing its big head on the chest of its master, who said, 'Please tell my cousin that I am very happy up here! I have refound my horse which I loved so much. I don't forget my friends, but I do not regret having left the earth."

The sitters were much impressed by this evidence. "It's extraordinary," the cousin said. "I never thought this was possible. I, above all, did not think animals could survive. My cousin, whom you are seeing, died of sadness after the death of his horse!"

Mediums have brought us a good bit of evidence for the survival of animals after death, not only by seeing pets who were recognizable to their sitters but by their own experiences when visiting in spirit realms.

Gladys Osborne Leonard, the British medium who died in 1968, wrote in her book *My Life in Two Worlds* (London, 1931): "An animal that you have loved and who has loved you, whether it be horse, dog, cat, or bird, goes usually to the third sphere where somebody takes care of it, and where it leads a normal animal life . . . and is even brought to see you at times while you are still on earth. I know you will meet your pets, the animal companions that you have loved. I have seen my special cats, and also a dog, a Pekingese, to whom my husband and I were much attached. It seems as if the animals who love, and are loved, attain the spiritual rights and have an afterlife in the spiritual world, just as we do. Whether their 'post-physical' lives continue forever, I do not know. I rather doubt it; this is, I doubt if they continue everlastingly in animal form, but they certainly live for a considerable time in the shape we loved and knew them by, and, thank goodness, they will live with us again when we pass over."

At the beginning of this book, I talked about my visits to the late Frank Decker, a controversial medium whose séances included startling physical phenomena. There, I met a couple who came every Tuesday to met their beloved dog who was "in spirit." In the darkened séance room, an animal shape jumped onto the couple's laps, raced between the chairs, and barked joyously. All I can say, is: I was there; I heard it all.

11. A New Beginning for Dr. Rhine?

In the ninth decade of his life, Dr. J.B. Rhine, the man who made ESP a popular concept the world over, proposes a fresh look at scientific research into life after death.

Rhine had stopped work on this problem some forty years ago, but he always regarded this action as an interruption, not an end to his efforts. Scientific discoveries are made by men, by individuals, even in this age of committees and computers. Dr. Jonas Salk gave us the polio vaccine; Dr. Christiaan Barnard pioneered the heart transplant. And so it is in parapsychology, after-life study included.

One reason for Rhine's lifelong interest in man's survival of bodily death can be found at the outset of his career. When young Joseph Banks Rhine entered college, he enrolled in a pre-ministerial course. And while he later abandoned an ecclesiastical career, he has often admitted that problems of religion remained vital to him long after he became doubtful of the traditional solutions. Later still, he began to find some suggestions of evidence for the basis of the ancient theology he had given up. Today, he often tells church groups that parapsychology is ready and able to provide scientific parallels for many traditional religious concepts—especially for the modes of communication: prayer depends on telepathy, seership and revelation on clairvoyance, physical miracles and miraculous healing are psychokinesis, and prophecy is precognition.

"Life everlasting" is a basic Judeo-Christian concept, and as such it is naturally shared with Islam. Other beliefs in continued human existence beyond bodily death, reincarnation included, are to be found in virtually all faiths, everywhere on this earth. Addressing himself specifically to the religions of the West, Rhine says: "Parapsychology has opened a scientific door with a method of investigating many religious beliefs. The approach can be very cautious and neutral to all speculations or ideological biases. It can be motivated by the purest concern of science to discover an unbiased answer." Parapsychology stands ready, in Rhine's view, to offer a scientific investigation of major religious concepts, such as life after death.

The fact of the matter is that Rhine started out by doing after-life research, but, after about ten years, found himself stymied. Even while still in college, he found training for the ministry "too barren" for a deeper understanding of human existence and values. As in the life of so many psychical researchers who later switch to less emotion-laden studies, Rhine's first fascination was with the subject he eventually abandoned: after the model of British investigators, he studied mediums who seemed to enable the living to communicate with the dead.

After a year at Ohio Northern University and a half year at the College of Wooster, Rhine gave up his pre-ministerial studies midway through his sophomore year, moved in the direction of science, then sought an escape into nature by choosing the life of a forester. Although he entered the U.S. Marine Corps in 1917, he made plans to enter the Michigan School of Forestry after leaving the Marines. He married Louisa Ella Weckesser in 1920, and together they studied biology at the University of Chicago, in order to have a solid background in forestry. To this day they live in the tree-studded countryside just outside of Durham, North Carolina.

It doesn't take much of a feel for what makes people tick to sense behind all this empathy for nature, biology and forestry a deep identification with the cycle of life; seed, growth, and the continuing self-renewal that perpetually raises questions about origins, destiny, and immortality. All their lives J.B. and Louisa Rhine have retained their awareness of all life and a strong affection for plants, animals, and people, which has surely helped them in their exploration of psychic abilities beyond man's own species.

The Rhines began their psychical research in earnest when they were working for their degrees in plant physiology. One year was spent at the Boyce Thompson Institute at Yonkers, New York. For another two years, they taught at West Virginia University. Switching careers from the recognized field of biology to the still far-out study of "parapsychology," with no university position in sight, was a major decision for the young couple. It was an area of science, yes—but one that was not in high repute and did not promise the tangible and i..tangible rewards that come with more solidly established academic disciplines.

The man who did most to change their lives was Professor William McDougall, F.R.S., the pioneer psychologist whose career had brought him from Oxford to Harvard (in 1920) and finally (in 1927) to Duke University in Durham. McDougall's book, *Body and Mind*, published as far back as 1911, was, according to Rhine, "a decisive influence in keeping us on the trail of psychical research." In it, McDougall had said that while British studies had not yet resulted in verifying life after death, they had "established the occurrence of phenomena that are incompatible with the mechanistic assumption." He was thinking about telepathy but also the study of mediumship, and the Rhines found it exhilarating to discover that "this great man himself had for years been active in the kind of research that seemed to us most worthwhile."

J.B. Rhine has fought many a battle in his day, and won most of them. He can be subtle, shrewd, tough, and persistent; and he has made enemies. But no one can deny that he has remained touchingly grateful and even humble in recalling the support McDougall gave him when the Rhines were resolved at all costs to find a field of research that would not entangle them in cobwebs of prejudice and rigid attitudes. Rhine put it this way: "Science, too, like formal religion, had for us lost much of its authority, especially because we saw that our biology teachers were less than objective about challenges to mechanism and the psychologists too over-reactive to anything suggesting dualism. But thanks to both professions, we had learned to rely on objective experimental methods for answers to such provocative questions. So the fact that both these (as all the other) professions wanted nothing to do with psychical research did not completely deter us; we think now we were fortunate in having acquired both a respect for scientific method and, as a consequence of our uprooted theology, an unsatisfied curiosity as to what man's nature really was."

J.B. and Louisa Rhine were positively oriented toward religion until college introduced them to the sciences. At that point they came to regard "supernaturalism as logically unacceptable." Psychical research provided them with a possible bridge between religion and science. They looked at the studies reported by the Society for Psychical Research, London, and found them interesting. The claim of possible communication between "an assumed spirit world and that of the living" suggested "proof of postmortem survival." They admired this effort as something that none of the major religions had ever made. It was an attempt to produce "verifiable, repeatable demonstrations of one of religion's major doctrines," survival of the human soul after death.

If such proof could be provided, the young research couple assumed, "the materialist theory would soon be dead." They were turning spirit survival into a question for scientific tests instead of a matter of faith. They were quite aware of the better-known critics of this approach. Rhine consulted the Wisconsin psychologist, Dr. Joseph Jastrow, for advice, having read his *Fact and Fable in Psychology*, which is very critical of psychical research. Best of all, the Rhines spent a year with Dr. Walter Franklin Prince at the Boston Society for Psychic Research, who was about as much a critic of his field as he was a proponent. There was at that stage much quicksand around, and the Rhines learned to step cautiously, with the vigilant Dr. Prince ever on the alert. Right on the Boston scene itself, the flamboyant and oft-exposed medium "Margery," wife of physician and surgeon, Dr. Le Roi Goddard Crandon, was receiving nationwide publicity. The Rhines recall that they were "more strongly repelled by the contradictory claims than attracted by the grain of truth that just might possibly exist in the Crandon séances and their physical phenomena of purported spirit origin."

After one year, the Rhines left the Boston community with more disillusionment than hope. But they found the work waiting for them with Professor McDougall in Durham more promising. In 1927 McDougall had founded a Department of Psychology at Duke University, and the Rhines set to work screening stenographic records of messages obtained from several mediums. This was more than just routine work, as a Detroit educator, John F. Thomas, had sent stenographers with specific objects to each medium, a novel form of "proxy" sitting. What had been planned as a semester's research became a lifetime career. Dr. J.B. Rhine joined the Duke staff, taught philosophy and psychology, then full-time psychology, but always remained free to continue psychical research, which then still largely meant mediumistic studies into life after death.

Whatever it was that the mediums had "felt" from the objects given to them could hardly have been picked up through any of the senses. Rhine now says, "Something beyond their known abilities seemed definitely to have been indicated." But where did this knowledge come from? Spirits? Discarnate entities? Or, directly from the objects the medium had been given to examine? This was obviously no way to prove the survival of human personality after death.

But if it wasn't knowledge supplied by spirits, where did it come from? Other researchers had, of course, considered alternate explanations before this, even back into the nineteenth century. Now, with McDougall's support, Rhine set up a Parapsychology Laboratory, and recalls that he was "able to carry out moderately successful experiments in telepathy and clairvoyance and to develop methods of improved control to make these tests as carefully controlled as the psychological laboratory at that stage could contrive."

However, Rhine's worst expectations concerning mediumship were supported when he undertook a series of ESP tests with Mrs. Eileen J. Garrett in 1934. He published a detailed report on these experiments, "Telepathy and Clairvovance in the Normal and Trance States of a 'Medium'" (*Character and Personality*, December 1934), which has remained a landmark in parapsychology studies to this day. To put it briefly, Rhine found that Mrs. Garrett's ESP abilities were at about the same level when she was in trance, supposedly under spirit control, as when she was quite herself, in a waking state. But even in this now classic paper, he wrote that to postpone "any consideration of the survival hypothesis is not at all to reject it."

Rhine did draw a firm bottom line under the mediumistic research that had preceded the Garrett experiments, saying that "the 'direct' approach (so miscalled) has failed, even though it has been in the hands of some of the ablest workers for over forty years." Either the problem is beyond us, he added, "or inadequate approaches and methods were used." At any rate, after-life studies were put aside, and numerous tests in ESP and PK (psychokinesis) were undertaken. The post-mortem survival idea was still in the back of the minds of the Drs. Rhine. It had originally been meaningful to both of them, "primarily for its implication of the transcendent nature of the *living* man." At that point they found the mediumship road at least temporarily closed, but the ESP research trail wide open. In the mid-1930s there was a disruptive flare-up inside Duke's Psychology Department about the appropriateness of ESP research. World War II further interrupted ongoing work.

Much, of course, has happened in the intermediate decades. PMS (Post-Mortem Survival) has now been in a deep freeze so long that few people actually remember that the Rhines started out with after-death studies, gave them up with some reluctance, although resolutely; but that they never discarded their possible potential. While studying current research in out-of-the-body experiences, deathbed observations, and other contemporary means of gathering "circumstantial evidence" on life after death, I began to wonder where Dr. Rhine stood on this still-crucial question today. He had discussed "The Question of Spirit Survival" in detail in the *Journal* of the American Society for Psychical Research (April 1949), saying that it is extremely difficult to see at present what a spirit personality could do through a medium that could not be explained as well or better by the powers now ascribable to the medium herself." The task of "proving survival," he added, "has been rendered enormously greater by the advances in the ESP and PK work."

"No one has ever yet been prepared with the necessary background on information to plan intelligently crucial experiments," Rhine said, "which would discriminate between spirit agency and its counterhypotheses," such as clairvoyance and telepathy. But Rhine established some criteria that might be used, such as "similar phenomena attributable to living individuals" that might be shared by the nonliving. He said that "along with the study of apparitions of the dead must go a comparably diligent search for similar cases of apparitions of the living, including of course the barely alive, the drugged, the entranced, and the like." Also, one might try "to set up appropriate conditions designed to evoke and foster spirit manifestations if possible without waiting for their spontaneous occurrence." We should, he said, "try to reach out to possible spirit personalities" and even "attempt to cultivate initiative and ingenuity on the part of the hypothetical spirit intelligences themselves."

On the basis of early experiments, later disappointments,

but an unquenched curiosity about post-mortem survival, Rhine has advanced even more recent ideas on the subjects. These, I fear, have been widely overlooked. Dr. Rhine himself only mentioned them quietly, in the modestly titled "Comments" section he occasionally publishes in the *Journal of Parapsychology*. Frankly, I had missed these suggestions myself until he drew my attention to them when I asked whether post-mortem studies might not now be moved out of the deep-freeze compartment.

In the March 1975 issue of the *Journal*, Rhine discussed "A New Method for the Post-Mortem Survival Problem," which might achieve "successful testing of old problems that have been shelved (or stalled) for lack of a method with which to attack them, as in the question of post-mortem survival (PMS)." He sees helpful advances in method and equipment. It is easier now to eliminate other elements and to zero in on what I, not Rhine, am inclined to call "soul residue" from the living personality. Rhine says, "With all the advances in equipment and methods now available we can well expect to find out what the entire psi or parapsychic side of life is like, how closely identifiable and how separable, if at all, from the rest it may be." Does any living creature really have *anything* deathless in its make-up that is reliably registrable? Rhine asks. "Why not," he says, "start with the 'guinea pig' approach?"

"We should forget," he says, "about such earlier aims as 'identifying' memories and other personal characteristics to verify the implied source of the medium's message." Rhine suggests, "Instead, let us fix *first-step* attention on the hypothetical communicator's most identifying signs of psi." He says that "in the beginning the aim would be to work with animal subjects to develop a design that would allow the long-range study of gradually lowered states of consciousness, only eventually approaching the terminal stages of life." It would be a reverse version of recent studies in the "origin of life."

If, in the process he outlined, psi elements fade away as the experimental animal's vital functions cease, "the evidence would finally lead to a negative conclusion. . . . If, however, there is some psi process showing continuity beyond the end of the signs of life in the body, this would challenge the method to its utter extremities."

Rhine adds: "It would start a new assault of science on a

major problem of the ages. Whatever the results might be
with animals, the method could be applied to man, at least to
terminal patients, but it can well be done incidentally with
anesthetized persons, either under medical treatment or even
better, with normal healthy volunteer subjects."

He reminds us, however, how long it has been taking to
trace the origin of life, and cautions that studying the other
terminus, dying, and possible after-life, is likely to be even
more complex, time-consuming, expensive, and exacting.
He adds: "Yet we can expect from the approach, I think,
at the very least, a definitive answer one way or the other in
the course of time. One little reliable sign of PMS as showing the extrabiological nature of psi, either in animal or
human subjects, that would stand out as clearly as its extra-
physical nature has done over the years, would electrify the
whole field of parapsychology as nothing ever has."

Dr. Rhine suggests it would be worth our while to settle the
question, firmly, either way. "What mankind really most
needs to know," he says, "is just what the origin, nature, and
destiny of the life principle is in all its fullness and potential,
whatever that may be. Illusion, however pleasant, could have
but low survival value or satisfaction, even for the lay world
today."

He concludes with these thoughts: "Yet we are still so vast-
ly ignorant about life and mind and their origin and functioning that I doubt that anyone has a reasonably close guess
(or rational inference) as to the great ultimate universal truth
about them. It is likely to be beyond present power to comprehend when and if eventually it is revealed to the sciences.
What matters most today, in any case, is that we faithfully
preserve the indescribably wonderful privilege of exploring
the question as well as we can, intelligently and responsibly,
along with the other great unknowns of nature and man, with
all the endless tireless reach of curiosity the expanding
sciences can command."

12. Meet Dr. Crookall!

I want you to come and visit Dr. Robert R. Crookall, because he is a man to whom all of us who take a serious interest in life after death owe a tremendous debt. He is now in his late eighties and lives in quiet retirement in the once-fashionable spa city of Bath in southwest England. His house can be found, after going through a labyrinth of side streets, on a road called Landsdown Road Mansions—but don't let the word "mansions" conjure up images of nineteenth-century British pomp and circumstance: like the man himself, the house is tranquil, overcrowded with the memorabilia of a long life, a comfortable place to talk and think. It isn't timeless, either; the inevitable changes of twentieth-century conveniences and inconveniences intrude, but you can hear bird calls as well as an angrily barking dog through the open window of Robert Crookall's study.

This scholar is the world's most persistent, almost compulsive, collector of stories dealing with evidence of man's survival after death. His files, probably the largest in the world, deal largely with what used to be called "astral projection," but has now been given the more elaborate label of out-of-the-body experience (OBE).

When I talked to Dr. Crookall, he was, in the eighty-eighth year of a busy life, just back from a long weekend in the country and in the midst of finishing a new book. His life reflects a consistent interest in "astral travel" that is certainly based on some form of indelible personal experience, but Crookall says he'd rather cite the research he has done, the cases he has collected, the conclusions he has drawn.

Scientists, notably those in professions where human emotion and experience play a role in career decisions, have found that life patterns and personality play an influential role in the direction of research. When I made this point to Dr. Crookall, he dropped some of his British reserve and provided glimpses into his background that had not been previously published. As a sturdy octogenarian, bald and 5' 8" tall, he strikes me as a man who surely has "nothing to fear" from the possible criticism of those who might find it odd that a scholar, distinguished in something as three-dimensional as geology and fossil research, spent much of his life "chasing ghosts in one form or another."

If he has one regret, Crookall says, it is that he loved music but never had the fulfillment of studying the piano under a professional teacher. His father had been a joiner (carpenter), and there had simply been no money in the family to pay for such frills as study of a musical instrument. The elder Crookall had to provide for four children, his wife's mother and sister, as well as two orphan boys left by his brother. "There was, of course, no government aid, in those days," Dr. Crookall says wistfully, "but I never heard my father grumble."

His appreciation of his father lasted beyond death; and this may be the acorn from which the strong oak of Crookall's fascination with life beyond death has grown. He recalls that, three years after his father's death, he "saw" him looking at him. This was during the interim stage between waking and sleeping when, Crookall says, "I get most of my experiences of this nature." It is also the period when, according to the Austrian-Swiss historian-mystic Rudolf Steiner—popularized by Nobel Prize winner Saul Bellow in his novel *Humboldt's Gift* (New York, 1975)—we can best have a dialogue with the dead. At any rate, Robert Crookall remembers that his father's gaze was directed at him "very intently, conveying a message which I well understood." Some psychologists, Crookall says, may regard such an encounter as a "memory image," but his vision of his father differed from any actual memory: "At his death, he was ill and worn-out looking, but when I saw him he appeared in the prime of life, actually quite beautiful and with a fine, straight nose. I had actually never seen him this way before; as a baby, he had been dropped on to a kitchen fender [a railing-frame before a fireplace], and his nose was out of shape, as a result of his accident."

Robert Crookall was born in Lancaster, England, in 1890. He studied chemistry, botany and psychology, and began his career as a lecturer in botany at the University of Aberdeen, Scotland. His special field was fossil plants, and in 1924 he was invited to join the Institute of Geological Sciences to engage in research in this particular area. His work included advising on new regions that might be opened to coal mining, on which he collaborated. The last of thirteen papers, dealing with "The Fossil Plants of the Carboniferous Rocks of Great Britain," was published in 1977.

Despite this demanding professional interest, Dr. Crookall retired in 1952, three years before the actual retirement date, in order to work in parapsychology. He now recalls that, "having had miscellaneous psychic experiences, I felt convinced that others had overlooked the value of some 'communications' as well as that of out-of-the-body experiences." By "communications," Crookall obviously refers to references made by alleged discarnate entities, either through mediums or other channels.

Being short of cash, Crookall did not marry until he was 38 years old. He has truly devoted a major part of his life to the investigation that he regarded as so very crucial. Since his wife passed on, in 1969, Crookall has lived alone. "I work as hard now as ever I did before," he says, "and if my memory is practically perfect, it's because I really attend to what I see or read, and my curiosity has remained undiminished." The Crookalls' son is a professor of engineering at the Cranfield Institute of Technology in Bedfordshire.

Recalling the work of the late psychic researcher, Hereward Carrington, on the out-of-the-body experiences of the American OBE forerunner, Sylvan Muldoon, Crookall says that Carrington "was sure Muldoon's 'astral projections' were genuine, although he himself had none." Crookall, who emphasizes that his personal experiences "are not for retail," says that he, too, deals with "evidence converging from separate sources, and all pointing at the same conclusion." He did not personally "obtain very definite details," such as have been related by Muldoon, Robert Monroe and others, because he found himself "differently constituted."

Dr. Crookall says: "My objective is not to persuade people to accept such propositions as out-of-the-body experience and survival after death, but to have them form their own, well-considered conclusions and—more important—to make sure, later on, that these insights affect their manner of living in the physical body. After all, our physical existence must largely determine a manner of living in our Subtler Body after physical death."

To Crookall, "Knowledge involves responsibilities, and to ignore responsibilities is to suffer consequences." He feels very strongly that people should "not try deliberately to project from their bodies." In other words, he is totally opposed to individual experimentation with out-of-the-body experiences. "If an experience comes naturally," Dr. Crookall advises, "well and good. But if it is forced in any way, it may—and I know cases in which this has actually happened—get out of control." It is one thing to open a "door" into the relatively unknown, such as an OBE, but, Crookall, warns, "it is quite another to be able to shut that door again, once it has been opened." He cautions particularly against forcing such experiences by using drugs; he calls this "the worst possible approach." As for those who enter the unknown and then perhaps unsuccessfully and desperately try to return to their physical body, Crookall makes the comparison that "a chick who emerges from its shell prematurely is subject to injurious forces."

Crookall's own research into communications with discarnate entities began as the result of a suggestion by Professor Henri Bergson (1859-1941), the French philosopher and one-time President of the Society for Psychical Research, London. Bergson felt that such communications "might furnish proof more logically cogent than is possible from mere access to earth-memories." He thought they should be examined "in the same sort of way as travelers' tales." Crookall's work in this field is the basis of his book, *The Supreme Adventure* (London, 1975). This work has been described by the Reverend George Whitby, a lecturer on the scientific method at two British universities, as having "a solid basis" and having "finally convinced" him of the reality of survival after death.

Having devoted so much of his life to survival studies, linked with out-of-the-body phenomena, Dr. Crookall has specific explanations for the fact that some individuals have particular detailed projections out of their bodies, while others do not; he says these differences "reflect their total body conditions." He explains: "Most people have vehicles of vitality, or 'vital bodies,' that are strongly immersed in their physical bodies and most of them are not morally or spiritually advanced: their 'super-physical' Soul Bodies are not organized instruments of consciousness—hence they have no satisfactory projections. The relatively few people who also have 'tight' vital bodies but who have organized them by moral and spiritual feelings, thinking and acting, tend to project the Soul Body only (and to glimpse Paradise), but, since there is a great vibrational 'gap' between their Soul Bodies and their physical bodies, they often remember nothing but a great inexplicable sense of peace; moreover, they do not have the experiences that are described by the few people who have a "loose 'vital body' ": this they project more or less readily, especially if they are ill."

Dr. Crookall adds: "A few people have a loose 'vital body' and this projects more or less readily, especially if they are ill, fatigued, affected by sedative drugs, or similar influences. As the 'vital body' is the bridge between the Soul Body and its physical counterpart, the double which they release is composite in nature: it consists of (a) part of the 'vital body' which enshrouds (b) the 'super-physical' Soul Body. However, almost always this composite double sheds the 'vital' element—passes through the second 'death'—and the Soul Body is un-enshrouded."

Dr. Crookall finds fault with psychologists who categorize out of the body "doubles" as mere "mental images," or as otherwise imaginary. He regards the concept advanced by the Swiss philosopher-psychologist, Dr. C.G. Jung, that such "doubles" are "archetypes" as "unacceptable." Crookall pits against such interpretations the "many cases of projection in which the double is released, and then returned to the body, in two separate stages." He adds: "No medical man or psychologist has taken note of the fact that mental images do not appear and eventually disappear in two stages."

Crookall defines the "double" as "the nonphysical body" which is "outwardly a replica, a double, of the physical." He uses the term "Soul Body" as describing something "superphysical" in nature, whereas "the vehical of vitality, by means of which the Soul Body contacts the physical body is 'semi-physical.' " These and other definitions are contained in his book, *The Interpretation of Cosmic and Mystical Experiences* (London, 1969). He also says in this work: "Physical death, so much dreaded by so many, is only an incident in a well-ordered and beneficent process, and only needs to be understood to be accepted with gratitude."

Crookall belongs to a generation that turned the things

that really mattered into an agreeable, though time-consuming hobby, an avocation rather than a vocation. His life's work, as we have seen, is in geology and mining; his scholarly papers appeared in such journals as *The Geology Magazine*, *The Annals of Botany*, and the *Proceedings of the Institute of Mining Engineers*; one paper was published in a periodical succinctly called *Fuel*.

Dr. Crookall is one of that nearly extinct species: the scientist who won't let scholarly methods get in the way of his imagination or curiosity. He wants us to be aware of what happens within and around us, and for that reason he wants us to step back and think about ourselves. His favorite comparison is the fact that, while we've been on this earth between one and two million years, we didn't even realize that blood circulates through our bodies until, to be precise, 1628. There are, Crookall says, other things happening within and without us that we still haven't really grasped, and it's about time that we did.

With the diligence of a pack of magpies, Crookall spent decades collecting case histories of "astral projections." He assembled hundreds of them, and has published them in such books as *The Study and Practice of Astral Projections*, *More Astral Projection* and *The Techniques of Astral Projection*. The trouble with, but also the value of, this type of material, is that it varies so little. One astral projection is pretty much like the next—that is, once you get used to the idea that your "soul" or "astral" self is actually capable of separating from the physical body and going on long or short journeys. Seeing one elephant fly is big stuff, but once it becomes an accepted and frequent procedure, no "Dumbo" will get us to turn around and give him a second look. This actually happened with the incredible, televised landings on the moon. The first time, when an astronaut made his "small step for man, but big step for mankind," we were all up at four o'clock in the morning; the final moon landing was just about fit for the six P.M. news, and few people paid much attention to it.

I asked Dr. Crookall whether, having collected thousands of out-of-the-body cases, he wasn't disappointed that the world hadn't beat a path to his door. He wasn't, but he welcomed the new wave of interest that OBE had aroused in the United States. He did draw my attention to the view he expressed in one of his latest books, *The Mechanics of Astral Projection* (Moradabad, India, 1968), where he said that "the fact that one is unaware of possessing a second body is no argument against its existence." Our ignorance is just as unimportant as our former ignorance about the vital function of blood circulation in the body.

And, of course, Dr. Crookall answers the question, "What does it matter?" with the strong suggestion that "it matters a great deal," and for this reason: "If a man can leave his physical body temporarily and continue to exist as a self-conscious being, the fact would provide a strong presumption that eventually, when he comes to leave his physical body, i.e., to die, he will then also continue to exist as a self-conscious being in that second body."

That, of course, is the argument which some modern researchers talk about as if they had just thought it up! Crookall has been giving the matter some thought for about seventy years, and he has heard just about all possible arguments, for and against. Robert Crookall is a kindly man, and he doesn't at all deny that some stories about "astral projection" may be fanciful, fiction, the result of some neurological deviation, or God knows what else. Much, he is well aware, happens in times of special stress. But other out-of-the-body experiences are, in his view, totally "normal" (he agrees that it's useless to argue the term "normal" outside some abstract psycho-medico-philosophical framework).

Dr. Crookall does recall, out of his vast collection of cases, some that have been sufficiently well recorded to be more than in the gee-whiz-I-can-hardly-describe-it pattern. He recalls a case described by the author William Gerhardi, in his book *Resurrection* (London, 1934) as "perhaps the most complete and convincing." It contains one element that Crookall calls the "silver cord," a link between the physical body and the separate, apparently nonphysical one. Gerhardi's experience started out in a most ordinary manner. He had simply stretched out his hand to switch off a table lamp. But just as he was about to press down to turn off the light, he found himself "suspended in midair." As he recalled it, he was "fully awake," quite startled and told himself, "Fancy that! Now would you have believed it! Now this is something to tell! And this is not a dream!"

At his point, Gerhardi found himself "seized and placed on my feet." He stood there, "the same living being." As he put it, "If the whole world united in telling me that it was a dream, I would have remained unconvinced." He added:

"I was in the body of my resurrection. "So that's what it is like! How utterly unforseen!" I staggered to the door. I felt the handle, but could not turn it. Then, turning, I became aware of a strange appendage. At the back of me was a coil of light. It was like a luminous garden-hose. It illuminated the face on the pillow, as if attached to the face of the sleeper. The sleeper was myself.

Who would have thought that I had a spare body at my disposal adapted to the new conditions! But I was not dead; my physical body was sleeping peacefully, while I was apparently on my feet and as good as before. "Now how will I get out?" I thought. ... At the same moment the door passed through me, or I through the door. I was in the corridor, dark, but illumined by a subdued light which seemed to emanate from my body. The next instant I had entered my bathroom, affecting from habit to switch on the light, but unable to press it down.

There was this uncanny tape of light between us like the umbilical cord, by which the body on the bed was kept breathing ... "Now, be scientific!" I said, "This is one chance in a million! You must convince yourself so that nothing later will make you think it was merely a dream!" All this I said to myself while going round and collecting such evidence as: that window is open; that curtain is drawn; this is the new towel-heater. I noticed a familiar outline of myself in the looking glass.

"What evidence? What more evidence?" I kept asking myself, as I passed from room to room. Here I noted which windows were shut, then I tried, and failed, to open the linen cupboard. Then I noted the time ... I flew through the front door and hovered in the air, feeling an extraordinary lightness of heart. Now I could fly anywhere, to New York, etc., to visit a friend, if I liked, and it wouldn't take me a moment. But I feared that something might happen to sever the link with my sleeping body.

What was I going to do now? "Proof," I said, I wanted irrefutable proof which would convince me and others when I came back into my body.... Whom could I visit? And at that moment the thought occurred to me: let me visit my friend Max Fisher at Hastings. Again I flew off ... Suddenly, I was stepping over an open patch of grass.... I thought, How do I know I am not dreaming this? And the answer,

"Look for the lighted cord behind you." I looked round. It was there, but very thin. . . .

Then, with a jerk which shook me, I opened my eyes. I was in my bedroom. Not a detail of my experience had been lost to my mind and there was quite another quality about it all, that of reality, which removed it from the mere memory of a dream. . . . We had a duplicate body all there and ready for use, the almost indistinguishable double of our natural body. It seemed that, for the first stage of survival at any rate, we already had a body, stored away, it is true, like a diver's suit, but nevertheless neatly folded in our everyday bodies, always at hand in case of death or for special use . . . I got up, and went through the rooms, checking the mental notes I had made about which windows were closed or open, which curtains drawn; and the evidence in all cases proved correct."

Gerhardi reasoned as follows: "If my body of flesh could project this other more tenuous body, while I could behold my flesh stretched out as if in death, then this subtler body, adapted to the subtler uses of another plane, was also but a suit or vehicle, to be in turn, perhaps, discarded for another . . . Gone was the notion that death was eternal rest. . . . Gone was the notion that the soul was like a little fleecy cloud. That twin body was real enough. Perhaps it was rash to think that conditions beyond the grave were entirely different from ours. The surprise might be that they were the same."

To the degree that art imitates life, and that fiction may elaborate fact in a manner that gives it depth and detail, it is worth citing one passage quoted by Dr. Crookall from Horace Anneleley Vachell's book *When Sorrows Come* (London, 1935). It is particularly intriguing, because the reaction of the protagonist so closely parallels that reported by physicians whose deathbed patients were actually resentful at being restored to life, because their glimpse of the world beyond death had been euphoric. Vachell's novel speaks of the train accident in which a woman, Joy, spoke to her husband, George, after she recovered temporarily and said, "I seemed to get away from my body. I saw my body, and I wanted to get away from it. And I was being borne along, wafted along."

Exactly as in today's OBE's, Joy reported that she felt she was being received, on "the other side," by her deceased mother, who took "hold of me." The account continues: "I was surprised. I couldn't hear her voice, but somehow I understood that I was not to be frightened. I wasn't, not a bit. And then I remembered what had happened when she died. She died, as you know, of heart failure. The nurse gave her oxygen and then the heart began to beat again. She opened her eyes, smiled at me and said, 'Why did you call me back?' She never spoke after that."

Certainly, the parallel of this fictional account—which may well have had its original in factual story told to the author—is striking, and makes it sound completely contemporary. In the novel, Joy continues as follows:

"The rest of my dream was wonderful. The mist seemed to clear and I saw three other persons. One was Cynthia Barclay [who had died previously]. I expected her to speak. Nobody spoke in my dream, but I understood what they wanted to say to me. Cynthia was unhappy about Alex [who had also perished in the train wreck]. She made me feel unhappy. I knew without her telling me that she wanted to help him and couldn't. Again, I wasn't surprised till I saw Harry Bignold. He appeared terribly distressed. I know, of course, that he was dead, but he didn't know it. A stranger to me was supporting him just as my mother was supporting me. Cynthia had gone. My mother made me understand that Harry couldn't realize he was dead. The man with him was Mr. Tarrant. I seemed to read Mr. Tarrant's thoughts. He was distressed about Harry and Mr. Dubois [another crash victim]. Then I found myself with mother. She made me feel that I had to go back. How did I get here?"

Fiction or not, this account is so close to the type of OBE report we have recently had from Dr. Moody and other researchers, that it rounds out what looks very much like a universal experience, certainly cross-cultural and of long standing. In the Vachell novel, Joy's husband, George, has a similar experience, leaving his body while in a sleep stage: "He could see his body on the bed and was glad to be quit of it. He felt extraordinarily light and happy. And then, turning from what lay on the bed, he saw Joy his wife."

At this point, the account gains a subtlety that few, if any, factual reports can achieve; and, possibly, the novelist's talent has added a dimension which we can only sense but not prove. In his OBE stage, George saw that Joy smiled at him: "He had a first impression that she had left her bed and had come upstairs to surprise him, fully restored to health. She looked so young and happy. She seemed to say, 'You are out of your body, George, and so am I. I had to come to you, as I did yesterday, because you are beginning to believe what happened to me was a dream. It wasn't a dream. I left my body after the accident. If you refuse to believe that, you will be very unhappy." The account then speaks of George in this manner: "He was to face her 'passing' with a firm faith that it would be well with him if he believed in their reunion. Light had come to him: he knew that Joy had 'passed over'; he knew that it was well with her. The nurse came in. 'She has gone!' she said."

Crookall maintains, and I think he must be right, that this story was much more than a "literary artifice." In the light of our current knowledge it stands to reason, as Dr. Crookall suggests, that the author had based it on actual cases Vachell had known. Crookall specifically draws out attention to these elements: the mother's reluctance to return to earth life, of which we have parallels in OBE's in operating rooms; the community of feeling between the living and the dead, whereby the dead share "our grief" for them; and the "superficially unbelievable statement that some of the dead are unaware that they are dead!"

While much modern research is done by teams or committees, in laboratories or with the help of full-time or part-time assistants, Dr. Crookall's valuable collection of hundreds of out-of-the-body experiences is the result of one man's total dedication of personal energy and financial resources. 'Because I bought thousands of books, rather than borrow them from a library and then forget their content, as many others do," Crookall says, "I never had a car, and I had to sell 3,-000 of them when I moved into my present flat." Below is a sampling from the Crookall collection. His method of classification and reference listing is probably unique. "I make my own index to each volume on the fly-leaf, as I proceed through each volume," he says. "Once this is done, I make my own alphabetical index, type two copies, and paste one copy in the back of each book." The following case histories, with Dr. Crookall's file number listed, are taken in excerpted form from his book *More Astral Projection*, with the author's kind permission.

Crookall received two experiences from Mr. Peter Urquhart of Rosedale, Toronto, Canada. The first case, conveyed in a letter dated November 19, 1961, mentions that he relaxed on a sofa and then had the following impressions:

Suddenly, and yet quite smoothly, I left my body. I was aware that all the natural processes—breathing, heartbeat—had stopped in my physical body, but I did not feel in the least worried since I knew that I was very much alive. After a time, I came back into my first body, but it felt a different shape—just in the way one notices by the feel if one puts on a different glove or hat than one usually wears.

After this I went outside and found myself out of the body again. This time the sensation was like being in a balloon, attached by a cord somewhere in the region of the navel, like the umbilical cord. It was a bitterly cold day in February, yet though I had my coat open and could sense the cold striking my [physical] body, it had no effect on me ["double"]. This latter fact struck me particularly, as I am usually sensitive to cold. There was a sense of exhilaration throughout the experience. Finally, a street-car came along which I had to take and the experience ended.

Upon receipt of this account, Crookall wrote to Urquhart and referred to his reference to something "like an umbilical cord," and asked, "Did you see this cord before or after you had read of it anywhere?" The reply, dated December 6, 1961, was as follows:

I quite appreciate the significance of whether or not the person has heard or read of these matters before experiencing them. In my case, I can say that after the first experience I realized what was meant in Ecclesiastes, by "the silver cord." At the same time, I had read that famous verse and it had remained in my mind, but until the experience I had not the slightest idea what it meant; it just seemed a poetic image. Certainly I had no idea that it referred to a link between body and soul, and I had no idea of this separation until I actually experienced it myself. As you know, these experiences bring their own authority and understanding with them, and when I had been out of the body I knew that if the "cord" was ever "loosed," I would be cut off from physical life—or dead, as we call it. . . .

Until I had some personal experience of such matters, I was rather a sceptic, regarded thoughts of personal immortality as "wishful thinking," and although I valued the Bible for some of its ethics and the beauty of its language, I had no idea that it contained a practical, inner meaning. In my case, theory came after practice . . . It seems to me that your work—the building up of a large body of evidence to show that these are quite normal experiences—is of great value.

A second experience was described by Urquhart (Case No. 371) as having taken place during a visit to England. His account states:

On this occasion a road which I crossed daily had been turned into a one-way street because of the Earl's Court Motor Show. I did not know this, and looked to the right automatically, saw that the road was clear, and stepped off—right into the path of a truck!

Actually I was throwing myself back instinctively before I had really seen the truck—and due to this, and very quick action on the part of the truckdriver, we missed collision by about two inches. It was so close that a policeman standing a few feet away said, "Did he hit you, governor? . . ."

The interesting part of all this occurred at the moment I turned and saw the truck on top of me. Immediately, I became aware of the second body; it was contiguous with the ordinary body and did not leave it, but I know it was separate and indestructible. A great calm was in me—the idea that Peter Urquhart was hit by a truck had no relevance. I know that I could not be hit by a truck. Time was superseded; although the truck was coming towards me at about 35 m.p.h., and a few feet away, it did not move. There was all the time in the world to see every detail of it . . .

My own conviction was that if I had been hit by the truck, my consciousness would have just remained in the second body. It had a definite feeling of materiality—though perhaps of a finer substance than we are normally aware of, it was a substance.

Back on the sidewalk, I noticed an unusual fact. Such experiences usually produce shock; there is tremor, accelerated pulse, heavy breathing, etc. as the body works off the accumulation of adrenalin. This time there was none of that; my body was as relaxed as if I had just risen from an easy chair.

I have had many other experiences which have proved to me, personally, the reality of the fact that we are more than three-dimensional creatures.

CASE No. 372—*Mrs. D. R. Lissmore*

Mrs. Lissmore of Hatfield sent this (Oct. 4, 1960): "When I was twenty-one, in the W.A.A.F., I had fallen deeply asleep. The girl who occupied the bed next to mine came in from a dance at 1 a.m. She had ice on her heels and slipped. As she fell, she brought her arm down across my chest with great force. When the blow fell it seemed to me that I was very far away. I could hear my body give a scream—not very loud because I was not there to give any power to it. I was not frightened, although my body screamed—I was too much occupied in getting back to take control of my body. It seemed that 'I' came rushing back through the darkness at great speed, took control, opened my eyes, and stopped screaming. ... Is this just the normal experience of a person suddenly awakened from a deep sleep, or does it have a deeper significance?"

[These cases should be compared with that of S. Bedford, mentioned in *The Supreme Adventure*, pp. 29, 87. Bedford told of a boy-friend who was nearly drowned: he stated, "As I touched the water I seemed to leave my body ..." A "communicator" told Bedford, "Our soul-consciousness is very much ahead of our physical consciousness. So, when instant death occurs through an accident, the Soul is aware of what is about to happen a split second before the impact occurs." Sir Winston Churchill had a similar experience in a car-crash.]

CASE No. 373—*Renée Haynes*

Renée Haynes (*Journal of the Society for Psychical Research* 41, 1961, p. 52) reported that racing motorists declared that, when driving at great speed, they "saw" themselves at the wheel, driving, while the physical body became identified with the car. We suggest that sudden, rapid movement of the physical body is not taken up by the "double" which therefore discoincides. Muldoon (1929) mentions sudden movements (e.g. stepping on a stair that "isn't there"), dervish dances, etc., as causing the release of the "double."

CASE No. 374—*Wm. T. Richardson*

Mr. Richardson (*Journal of the Society for Physical*

Research, 41, 1961, p. 214) made a similar observation in connection with aeroplanes. He said, "Disassociation of mind with the physical world is apparently a fairly common phenomenon experienced by pilots, particularly those who fly at great heights and speeds. This sensation of 'out of body' is a momentary experience of detachment, a glimpse of oneself as though from without. Not only have I had such an experience, but others sharing the common background of solitary flight have told me of their experiences with similar sensations."

CASE NO. 375—*Samuel Woolf*

Mr. Woolf, of Chicago, Ill., U.S.A., sent the following (Sept. 5, 1961): "While in Denver very recently I received a copy of your book *The Study and Practice of Astral Projection* and found it very stimulating. I did read *The Projection of the Astral Body* (by Muldoon) about two years ago. In it I found the answer to the question which had been bothering me for many years. Previously I knew nothing about occultism, etc., because, due to my life-time deafness, I was practically isolated from many things which I am learning at the present.

"In 1932 my parents and I were in Wisconsin for a few days. One dark night I was walking with my mother on the left side of the road back to our hotel and a car swerved far to the left, hitting me in the right thigh. All of a sudden, I went through the sensation of a locomotive ploughing into me. I [from the released 'double'] saw my figure on the ground struggling to get up for a few seconds and then I found myself getting up. It was ten feet away when I [from the 'double'] saw my own body getting up. So for many years I wondered why I saw my own body—and I found the answer in the book."

CASE NO. 377—*Mrs. G. W. Dew*

Mrs. Dew, of Ditton Hill, Surbiton, wrote the following to the [London newspaper] *Daily Sketch* (Oct. 11, 1960):

"My husband was seriously wounded with shrapnel on Nov. 4, 1941. One piece went right through the right leg, one was in his wrist, and one in his neck, close to the main artery.

"He regained consciousness and told the others how to

bandage him up. He was taken down to the base hospital and clearly remembers floating about five feet up, looking down on the doctors and nurses as they operated on him."

CASE No. 370—*Miss Marion Price*

Miss Price said: "In August, 1957, I was hurrying and fell down our long flight of stairs. On the way down I experienced a quick review of all the chief events of my life. There seemed plenty of time and no hurry, and it seems to me that someone or something asked me if I wanted to go on living? I was quite myself and . . . said a definite 'Yes!' Then this other (whatever it was) told me to strike out with my right arm, which I did, as it were, swam round the bend to the bottom of the stairs, falling on my right side. I was very shaken and the doctor put a stitch in my head. It occurred to me afterwards that if I had not followed the injunction and struck out to the right, I should have struck the wall before the bend with my full weight on the top of my head, which would probably have killed me. What amazed me afterwards was to think of the short space of time I must have been in actually falling, and yet the clarity of the life-review and the clear question and answer on the way down."

Crookall finds himself in disagreement with Dr. Jean Lhermitte, of the Paris Academy of Medicine, who published an article, "Visual Hallucinations of the Self" in the *British Medical Journal* (1951, pp. 431–34). Now, Dr. Lhermitte, is an extraordinarily experienced and creative neurologist who has made a lifelong study of the delicate borderline between what appear to be actual paranormal or psychic (parapsychological) phenomena, and neurological conditions that seem to imitate such phenomena; his work in "demonic possession" and pseudo-possession is one of unrivaled sophistication. We must therefore regard Lhermitte's view on the matter with care and respect. Lhermitte's study cited passages from the works of such writers as Edgar Allan Poe, Fyodor Dostoevsky, Gabriele D'Annunzio, Oscar Wilde, John Steinbeck, and others as "doubles" that were merely mental images of physical bodies. He cited Aristotle as speaking of a man who, when he was walking, approached him, and turned out to be himself. Lhermitte cited such cases as fiction devices designed to "stimulate the reader's imagination by showing him the strangeness of life and the complexity of the human mind."

While it is true enough that authors make up stories, it is equally true that their raw material is very often their own, and highly personal experience. People who are reluctant to admit having unbelievable things happen to them, may feel free to place them into the mold of "fantasy" and thus get rid of the emotional pressure built up by the experience, but also escape being stamped irrational by attributing the experience to another, fictional character. Being gifted at narration, we might get a more fully founded account of an OBE in a novel than from some tongue-tied, semiliterate OBE subject, frightened out of her wits, and barely able to utter a coherent sentence.

But back to Dr. Crookall, surely the world's leading researcher-historian of out-of-the-body experiences. It is his belief that "astral projection, and not space travel, is by far the most interesting and important phenomenon known to man." If you think you haven't had an OBE yourself, don't be so sure. Crookall has found that out-of-the-body experiences aren't rare; it is the memory of them that fails to cross the bridge into our conscious, everyday self. So you may very well have been an astral traveler, but simply do not remember it.

13. Ingo Swann Speaks His Mind

Probably the most consistently productive subject of out-of-the-body experiments is Ingo Swann, the New York artist whose abilities have been tested by the American Society for Psychical Research and at the Stanford Research Institute. At the ASPR, Swann has been a research subject of Dr. Gertrude Schmeidler, Psychology Department, City College of New York, and of Dr. Karlis Osis, who conducted the Society's long-range study concerning survival of the human personality after death.

Swann is unique in many ways; he combines an artistic career with his psychic testing work, while also writing works of fiction as well as nonfiction. His autobiographical work *To Kiss Earth Goodbye* (New York, 1975) was described by Jule Eisenbud, M.D. in *Theta* magazine (Summer, 1976) as placing the author "in the front rank of the current crop of psychic luminaries." Swann has broken with the long tradition of most psychic subjects who submit themselves, more or less passively, to test methods and conditions developed by psychic researchers; in a number of instances he has made striking alternate suggestions which proved that a vocal, intellectually versatile psychic may add dimensions to research projects that might otherwise remain unexplored.

The following questions were put to Ingo Swann by the author of this volume; they are reproduced here, unedited, in order to allow Mr. Swann full scope for the expression of his views.

Are you personally, or as a researcher, concerned with the question of the survival of the personality after death? If so, in what terms?

Of course I am, personally. Isn't almost everyone? I have found very few people who are totally unconcerned about their eventual destiny when the ugliness of death finally comes around to them. As a researcher, however, I have not felt creatively impelled to carry this concern over into research, for at least three reasons. First, I feel singularly ill-equipped and ill-prepared to undertake the enormous quanta of work and time that would be required for such an effort. Second, there are already researchers who have embarked upon various aspects at the present time, and who are studying first-hand and at close quarters the actual event of death. Third, I feel that any significant study of death and possible after-death existences will end up as more a political polemic than as any speedy conclusion favorable to the possibility of life after death.

Research, at the present, must be conducted within the constraints of rational empiricism. In one way, I see no need to hastily set aside this approach, since it has given humanity more science in the last 100 years than in the last 10,000. The scientific approach is goverened very zealously, however, and sometimes dictatorially, by rational materialists who decreed and cling to the hypothesis that there is nothing beyond physical interactions. The question of survival, therefore, has been vigorously opposed, often with such psychological violence as to be irrational and unbelievable.

The biggest problem, in a research sense, is the existence of this intractible paradigm, a rational materialism that seems to rest on the false assumption that there is nothing beyond the material. Most scientists know by now that this is quite untrue, and, where it is yet vigorously insisted upon, quite foolish. Quantum mechanics and recent observations concerning quantum inter-connectedness, surely indicate that, at the very least, the exclusion of nonmaterial facts can no longer be a desirable stance within science.

Yet, full and general acceptance of nonmaterial interactions in the psychological sense will entail a scientific revolution *par excellence*. This, to me, constitutes the larger problem. It is quite formidable. So I see this as a socio-political belief situation that involves powerful, if not respected, scientists who can not yet manage to bend their brains and personal realities to include the implications of trans-sensory phenomena.

I have therefore excluded, in a research sense, the question of survival from the work in which I have been involved. This is merely an economy of time and effort, though. Perhaps if, some time in the future, I can see an edge where profitable research might be accomplished without wasting vast amounts of effort on the diatribes of the outgoing material paradigm, I might take it.

Do you have a "mind-reach" image of life after death? Can you describe it? Can the average person conceive of it? Is it anything like the image that spiritualists have of the after-life?

I feel that everyone has an image of life after death, even those who deny it openly. My observations, which of course are not very scientific, lead me to the conclusion that everyone feels that they are immortal. At some level of awareness, however deep, dark hidden, or unconscious, this reality pervades all living beings. Where it is protested as a reality, there exists some curious psychological phenomena. I have observed at least two associated psychological states in the vigorous protesters of immortality. They are generally afraid of themselves as immortal beings. And sometimes it seems it is as if they don't want others to be immortal. And thus they must destroy any clues to immortality. I am not the only one to have come to this conclusion. This constitutes a first stage of psychic warfare, and is sort of an insidious psychodrama with intense psychopathological symptoms that has rampaged throughout recorded human history.

Now I have, of course, some sort of a mind-reach image of life, not one of life after death, but an image of life that includes death within it. It is difficult to explain. Science simply does not have any sufficient definitions of life or death at all. Material science is singularly ill-equipped to define life and to define death. The most that can be said is that, in the one, some bits of hitherto inanimate matter have been gathered into a biological organism that somehow animates itself. This is life. Death is when that organism lies slimy and rotting, and is obviously unlikely to be further animated. This is the best that material science can say about either life or death. Materialists have my sympathies here, since it surely must be quite difficult to concoct any really informative scientific rationales based upon what can be observed about physical life and death.

When material scientists submit bits of life to increasing penetration by electron microscopes and the such, they are rather embarrassed to find that at some point the animated matter sort of just disappears into a nonmaterial condition, is no longer there, but yet is still obviously there.

Now, from my point of view, a great deal of confusion comes from the scientific fact that scientists are not at all certain just what dies when something turns up dead. In my realities, physical bodies just simply do die, and so death seems to be a function of life. I feel that this is more likely so than, for instance, that life is a function of death. But this is hard to talk about, and usually results in a diatribe. This resembles another either/or conflict currently raging in science today. There are those who firmly hold that life is animated by electric parameters. These are called the "drys." A conflicting opinion holds that life is animated by chemical parameters. Those who believe this are called the "wets." These wets and drys are having a good time trying to undermine each other, amidst volleys of mutual insults.

Now, I think the average person can get ahold of this quite easily if he asks himself who is running his or her body. I don't think they would usually mistake their heartbeat for themselves. They can easily see that they are existing in a body, and probably doing a great deal to move it around, cause it to do things, and otherwise animate it. If some feel their body is running them, then they are already dead, or certainly shall be soon—sort of zombies roaming around, bemoaning the mortality associated with the limiting parameters of materialism.

I have spent at least fifteen years doing in-depth studies of spiritualism and spiritualists. I feel that only the uninitiated researcher could have much enthusiasm for the results of spiritualism. Spiritualists have, I think, established the existence of other realms of existence beyond the known physical. There are many excellent case histories that have checked out just too well to deny their validity. But the overall picture of afterlife established by spiritualists seems to constitute a vast universe where the disembodied wail and roam around, quite in shock over their disembodied condition. Only a small minority seems to constitute disembodied beings who wish to inform and help humanity. In fact, from my notes and collection over the years, I am slowly preparing a book that identifies the masters and so forth and compares their messages. And I must say that here I should join the ranks of the rationalists eagerly, since the conflicts and arguments and philosophies from the other side leave me somewhat at odds. Only the obvious clues that we can transcend death is encouraging.

You are familiar with the earlier efforts to establish man's immortality through mediumistic channels. Researchers such as Dr. Rhine maintain that we cannot prove survival in this manner. Do you agree?

Yes and no. As I said before, what actually constitutes "proof" is the real argument, not either the quantity or the quality of evidential communications. When the scientific demands and biases shift a little, I think much that has gone before will be reevaluated favorably.

Do you, as a "psychic" find usefulness in tools of contact with the dead, such as the Ouija board, various forms of automatisms (automatic writing)?

I make little effort to contact the dead. And, based upon my lengthy researches into these occult methodologies, I find very little to recommend them, except as entertainment. I am not the first to hold this view, though. Many, many spiritualists and occultists have recommended caution in any of this. There appears to be something about contacting the dead that can be deadly.

Have you personally encountered the dead? If so, can you give us one or several examples? Please, be as detailed as possible. Most of these accounts are fragmentary and badly described by the observers, or just trivial.

When my paternal grandmother passed on in Colorado, and I was fifteen years old, my family lived in Utah. That night, I remember, was one of those lovely evenings, with the marvelous sunsets that always burst over the Great Bonneville Valley. I had been outside, and just turned to go into the house, when, in the wind by my ear, her voice clearly said: "I have passed on in great pain, but it is over now!" I had never heard her more happy. Consequently, when, about an hour later, the telephone rang to tell us of her death, I didn't even cry. I was very impressed by this. She had died of stomach cancer, very painfully, and I fully understood that she was glad it was over, at last.

In the case of my maternal grandmother, she was put in a nursing home because of some sort of senility. She had led a good and full life, and all this seemed a shame. Yet, one evening, in my loft in New York, I was washing a Carnival glass plate she had once given me. She seemed ever so near. I said, "Say something." And she said, "I'm really dead, you know." I said, "I thought so, but give me a sign."

Something hit my hand, and the beautiful Carnival glass dish went up into the air and crashed to the floor, in about three dozen pieces. I was horrified. But I could hear her laughing. So, I feel this grandmother left her body long before it died physically. Soon after, one evening I was watching television, I thought she said in my mind, "I really am on my way now." So I telephoned my mother and told her I thought Grandma was dead. And she called the nursing home where they went to check the bed, and Grandma had passed on in her sleep, or at least her body had.

At other times, various ghosts have roamed through my existence. I usually encourage them to keep right on moving.

Have you, in any sort of "state," ever traveled into the realm of the dead?

Yes and no. First of all, I don't think there is any such place. There is a realm of dead, rotting corpses, of course, dried up things, occasionally put into expensive coffins and crypts. I think sometimes those beings ardently attached to their former bodies hang out there, real spiritual necrophiles. But in the psychic sense, being "dead" is a state of mind, if anything. This state of mind can be held by a psychic being living in a body, and so certainly can also sometimes be characteristic of someone who really is *sans* body, temporarily.

I think we have to redefine our premises here, a scientific and psychological action that won't be easy. I would have to say that if you could define the realm of the dead I might be able to tell you if I ever visited it. The answer would probably be yes, but since I think that the dead/life syndrome is a useless reference; I hesitate to say much more.

I might have to submit that in order to visit the realms of the dead, you must also be able to visit the realms of the living. This is almost as hard as contacting the dead, perhaps even more difficult. Just because people experience warm, palpitating, sweating bodies around or in front of them does not prove they have contacted a living entity. We are more likely to contact an image the living entity wants us to be impressed by. But this is just an image, not the living being itself. A little insight, psychological expertise, and intuition helps one dig deeper, and then it may be found that sometimes people (life) aren't what they appear. I think the living entity depends a great deal on the proportions and impact of the physical body to deliver a lot of his messages and living attributes. When this body lies dying, dead or decomposing, I feel that the being's images are probably scrambled up a little. So I think that all this is very messy, I try to keep out of it if I can.

There are a great many research reports of those clinically dead coming back to life, who report very cogently on their deathly experience. I would have to assume therefore that a certain proportion of dying people do maintain in good order their psychic and perceptual capabilities. But these examples appear to be in the minority, since the majority report just blackness and nothing. And I can easily see that where one has died, and is watching the mop-up operations of the physical body following death, and then zinging off into the clouds, where he might think he was now an ascended master. And perhaps he would be right.

The OBE is regarded by some as one of the categories of circumstantial evidence in survival studies. Do you share this view?

Yes, most certainly. I think, though, that the quality of the experience should be judged differently than it usually is, since it is really not known whether the being is in the body in the first place. I suspect he is not, ordinarily, and in the so-called OBE, he just shifts the focus and locus of his perceptual faculties. But, generally, OBE is a step in the right direction.

I am under the impression that you couldn't care less about such categories as OBE, traveling clairvoyance, telepathy, etcetera. Aren't these useful in keeping various forms of ESP separate from each other, to the degree that this is possible?

These terms were useful in the last century. Today, inspection of general psychical aptitudes has gone quite beyond them, and we need to start using expanded and more precise words. Take clairvoyance, for example. We can't really crowd all the following into it with any good advantage: psychic viewing of: a spinal cell, the interior of a heart, a cancer in the neck, an illness in another's body, the condition of a bioelectric field around a flower, a building 3,000 miles away, a typewriter in the next room, an oil deposit 6,000 feet down, something that is going to happen in the future, something that happened in the past, several ghosts, etc. What does a general term contribute to all these different aspects? No, we need new words, new terms, and a general refurbishment of ESP in the first place, as well as an updating of what has happened in psychic research, contrasted to directions that should now be established. Five old-fashioned words are simply useless.

Do you hold an opinion of the deathbed studies (Osis, Moody, etcetera)?

I certainly do hold an opinion, and it is a very fine one at that. These men and women (including Kübler-Ross and Roll) are very courageous and have my highest enthusiastic commendation. Their work is the best we have, since it is up to now the only work. Perhaps, in future, more precise efforts will come about. But these few have started something that should have been begun with the age of science, but wasn't for some inexplicable reason; well, not so inexplicable at that, if one takes into account my reference to first-stage psychic warfare.

Please tell us about your "mind-reach" work, whether or not it has significance, in your opinion, to afterlife research.

All the so-called "mind-reach" work in which I have been involved, from my point of view, has been toward discovering, developing and understanding living perceptual potential. If it has afterlife potential, then it is merely a by-product.

Do you care at all whether there is life after death, your own, or anyone's?

I feel, as I said earlier, that death is a function of the material universe, and life is a fact of some other universe that has not been researched here on earth. The laws of thermodynamics appear to insist upon conservation of energy through change. Thus, life and death in the material sense. There is something else, though, and it is only material stupidity and bias that stands between us and a more firm grasp of it.

Most people contact this other, each in their own way, and simply play dumb when the materialistic philosophy heaves its weight around, if they are smart, and try to challenge it, at other times. I do care, and deeply so, both for myself and all those others who feel trapped in the physical universe without certainty and understanding of their trans-physical capabilities.

If "mind-reach" can bridge gaps between physical points, can it also jump into other dimensions? Can it possibly reach extraterrestrial areas and/or personalities, including possibly the dead of the past?

Probably. But when, in future, these realities are laid out with their supporting evidence, you might not be able to ask these questions in the same way. I feel many people already do these things. In the overall gestalt of mind being interconnected with the rest of the universe, various data sort of leak into material consciousness once in a while. But, because we are not taught how to interpret these psychic events, rather unusual connotations are attributed to them.

What should future research in the general "*psi*" area seek to accomplish? What afterlife research do you foresee?

In the near future at least, the dramatic, fantastic and interesting aspects of *psi* may not be as important as some aspects having to do with the politics in science involving *psi*, and certain sociological and cultural shifts that I feel are necessary before *psi* can advance generally. One of the most important of these overall situations involves a general redefinition of what *psi* is. It most certainly is *not* just psychokinesis (PK) and clairvoyance/telepathy. The Eastern European concept of *psi* now goes under the term "psychotronics," an umbrella word that includes man as a bioelectric organism to a system of long-wave potentials, man as capable of participating in and with quantum interconnectedness, and man as a thinking, creating function, whose thinking and creating can be manipulated, formed and deformed by anything from DNA genetic alteration to overt mind control.

Here in the United States, especially, our parapsychologists sit around, aheming and hahaing, as to whether or not any given observed *psi* functioning is telepathy or may be clairvoyance. I do feel American parapsychologists have made many startling and magnificent breakthroughs, but generally their cultural attitudes have prevented these discoveries from taking a more significant place in the general scheme of culture. No amount of words can convey my disgust and sick disappointment, through the years, as I have witnessed and heard the diatribes and kindergarten-like battles and attacks that go on among parapsychologists themselves, much less those disgusting scenes between parapsychologists and science.

This dismaying cultural state of affairs in the field of *psi* can exist to the degree it does only because in the United States parapsychology in general has no broad or penetrating grasp of the meaning of *psi*.

Psi, as a new definition, would be seen to encompass all of man that is not distinctly material and following the laws of the physical universe. Those aspects of man that transcend physical expectations and limitations should be called psychic, or psychotronic. In fact, almost anything else is now unthinkable. The common materialistic cliché that everything is material, and if some things are not now understood that way, they will be so understood someday, will really no longer serve either man or science, and in fact is now a cliché that is totally irrational. Quantum mechanics, quantum inter-connectedness, synchronicity, telepathy and remote-viewing all attest to the existence of man's psychic nature. We should also include intuition, creativity and aesthetics into a new formal definition. And I don't think we should fail to include also those psychic ramifications known as brainwashing, mind-control, behavior modification, psychology in general (since aside from its physically related aspects, it too has a psychic nature), and certain forms of psychic warfare.

Most specifically, I think a great deal of thought needs to go into why psychic functioning is now a rational expectation rather than being arbitrarily declared as irrational. This constitutes a political lobby to be sure, but it is one that needs to be undertaken on behalf of all those scientists, and they are very numerous, who are trying to get a little research done in this area. Their research is impeded, often deliberately I feel, by having to apologize to their colleagues, to defend their right to do basic research free from harrassment, and in some cases fearing for their jobs. This dismal situation needs to be changed. Today science is great and grand enough to be able to winnow out the frauds and the ill-founded hypotheses. And since this is so, slobbering diatribes against psychic research appearing in the press, or behind the scenes to get possible funding cut off, are no longer in the best interests of science or mankind in general.

If some such cultural shift in definition does occur, I feel it will be easier to see man as a psychic/material organism, a sort of being that is more psychic than material, but which obviously is in great interaction with the material universes. I am suggesting this new approach not simply because I am tired and bored with the either/or situation as it exists between the so-called Spiritualists and the so-called materialists. But because I think by now the facts warrant it. Spiritualists, how ever etheric and spiritual they may be, are still operating out of and through a physical body, and, indeed, beings from the beyond often need someone else's body to communicate through. And the materialists, slavishly trying to conform everything to material constraints, are still cogitating methodologies to do just that. This spooks versus the rocks attitude should really end now, since honest appraisements of facts suggests that psychic/materialism is the next rationalism dawning.

As to afterlife research, I feel too much attention is devoted to this. This is probably because everyone does worry about what is going to happen when they find themselves enfolded in the soft feathers of death. This is too bad and I wish more people could face this coming attraction with certainty. I somehow feel that if people more conscientiously and with more interest examine *Life*, their apprehensions concerning the beyond will shift accordingly. They will perhaps find and accept that death, in the physical sense, is a conservation of energy principle. But, in the psychic sense, it is a state of mind, and probably a voluntary one at that, quite capable of being changed by the very one who possesses it.

14. To Know God's Will

The discussion of man's immortality has been taken over by scientists, including psychiatrists and parapsychologists. But what happened to the original basis of this concept in Western civilization: religion? In preparing this book, I decided to turn to one clergyman who stood at the crossroads of religion and psychical studies, the President of Spiritual Frontiers Fellowship, the Reverend L. Richard Batzler of Frederick, Maryland. I had met the Reverend Mr. Batzler at several get-togethers of the Fellowship, which I attended as some-time editor of its quarterly journal, *Spiritual Frontiers*, and as a speaker at its conventions and retreats. But, as such occasions usually dictate, we never had much opportunity to discuss questions of mutual interests in depth.

And yet, from various hints, I had gained the strong impression that Batzler had a more than average commitment to the concept of life after death. In some of his letters to me I detected this commitment; I became convinced that this impression was correct when I studied two booklets he had written, notably "Through the Valley of the Shadow," in which he advised fellow clergy and others in the task of helping to "cope with some of the practical everyday challenges and concerns of being with the dying." He based his comments on "psychological and theological studies" and "personal experience in ministering to the dying in hospital and home." In many ways, I felt, his thoughts paralleled those expressed by Dr. Elisabeth Kübler-Ross, although clearly within a ministerial framework. Batzler specifically suggested: "Share your own thoughts and feelings about death with [the] patient if you feel it is indicated. This includes your belief and faith in life after death."

I am well aware that a priest, minister or rabbi may have personal difficulty in accepting the concept of life after death, despite traditional and theological concepts of immortality. It is easier to speak of "faith" than to maintain it; our generation lives in a period of crumbling foundations and cracking pillars of religious convictions. When, therefore, the opportunity arose to ask the Reverend Mr. Batzler directly, and with as much candor as good taste would permit, just how he had arrived—if, indeed, he had arrived—at the conviction that life after death is a fact, I posed a series of probing, personal questions on this matter. The following is part of a transcript of this conversation.

EBON: It seems to me that as President of Spiritual Frontiers Fellowship you must, or should, have a particularly strong commitment to the idea of man's life after death. After all, the Fellowship has three basic areas to which it devotes itself. One is prayer; the second is healing; the third, and possibly foremost, is man's continued existence beyond death.

BATZLER: That's correct. First of all, I came into touch with Spiritual Frontiers by way of spiritual healing; and this, in turn, led me toward survival studies. It was a gradual process, a form of personal evolution.

EBON: Does that mean you went into SFF, in the first place, because it provided a sort of resonance to your own interest in spiritual healing?

BATZLER: Yes. (But let me back up a minute.) My own entry into the ministry itself took place after an earlier career in rather demanding, and at times stressful, government work. There's the old saying, "physician heal thyself." I started by having to come to terms with myself: to experience healing before I could, myself, be active in it.

EBON: What were the actual steps you took?

BATZLER: As I recovered from the emotional crisis that this career conflict brought with it, I made the personal commitment to enter seminary and make the ministry my life's work. The decision itself was part of the healing process. It was a major emotional transition.

EBON: At what point in your life did this happen?

BATZLER: I was in my mid-thirties. I was at the same time completing my doctoral thesis at Georgetown University in Washington, D.C. Thus, six years in government service were followed by three years in Seminary. And the minute I entered the ministry, I felt a very strong call toward spiritual healing; I came to understand it as central point of the New Testament mandate. And so I began holding healing services in the church.

EBON: Where was this?

BATZLER: In Baltimore. My denomination was the United Church of Christ. This was in the family tradition; The United Church of Christ, formed in 1957, was a merger of two different Protestant traditions, the Congregational-Christian and the Evangelical and Reformed. The Congregational Church was the church of the Pilgrims who broke away from the Anglican Church. The Christian Church was formed from several small American denominations. The Reformed Church had its origin in Germany and Switzerland and took its main form under Ulrich Zwingle in Switzerland. The Evangelical Church originated in Germany as a merger of Reformed and Lutheran.

EBON: At what point did your healing ministry become a really active part of your life?

BATZLER: This was in the early sixties. While I was serving the church in Baltimore, I became acquainted with the remarkable spiritual healing being done by Ambrose and Olga Worrall. [The late Ambrose Worrall, together with his wife Olga, have been leading figures within the healing and psychic studies movements in the United States for several decades.] At that point, the Worralls were also very close to Spiritual Frontiers Fellowship; they were the first to draw my attention to the work the Fellowship was doing, and I immediately felt an attraction to its activities.

EBON: Specifically, what role did the Worralls play in your affiliation?

BATZLER: They actually encouraged me to get into SFF. I had been fortunate enough to get to know them through the healing ministry. My church then was St. Paul's—United Church of Christ, in Baltimore. I organized Healing Services in the church, supplemented by pastoral counseling and referral services. I tried to make it a holistic ministry, using not only healing aspects in a formal service, but also trying supplementary forms of therapy.

EBON: How did SFF help with this?

BATZLER: In SSF I met other clergy, saw what other churches were doing. It gave me a chance to examine other forms of healing ministry, such as meditation and prayer, which expanded my own concept of healing. This was coupled with my continuing New Testament studies, such as the healings by Jesus, and viewing it against the background of my personal experiences and those that I had an opportunity of observing. Out of about one-hundred parishioners, several were actively involved in the healing work; there was no opposition to it, but a good deal of indifference. On the other hand, some people from the community around us were drawn to this aspect of our work.

EBON: People write to newspaper columnists, such as Ann Landers, and often the advice is to go and see your clergyman. Doesn't that put you into difficult positions sometimes?

BATZLER: Sometimes. More often such persons go to see the psychiatrist, who in a sense represents the new priesthood. People might not come to me with their emotional problems, but would be quite ready to talk to a psychiatrist. Even though referrals at first were few my interest in spiritual healing continued to expand within what I might call the larger community, a nation-wide community, which Spiritual Frontiers Fellowship represented. And this, in turn, got me into a deeper study of survival.

EBON: How?

BATZLER: This was an area which, until then, had been primarily academic with me, as it surely has been with many others, inside and outside the clergy. It had remained theoretical. But now, as I talked to people, sat in groups with them, and actually observed and experienced what to me was evidential in quality—this influenced my attitude greatly. Primarily, this came in sittings with the Worralls in their "Quiet Time" period of spiritual introspection and communication.

EBON: How did healing and survival come together?

BATZLER: I observed in what the Worralls did that at times there seemed to be actual influence from discarnate entities who helped them in their healing activity. I didn't experience this in my own work, but I always had a sense that there was "help" coming from beyond, and I have even more of a sense of this today.

EBON: But there is a crucial question of concreteness here. How strong was, or is, your feeling that your own healing power—presumably divinely inspired, provided, or aided in separate form a more directly guided healing faculty that originates with entities, whom you might call angelic, discarnate, or whatever is the suitable category?

BATZLER: This I cannot answer. I haven't come to that point yet. I am in the process of trying to evaluate this aspect further. Nothing specifically has come through me. In one instance, something that seemed very significant to me, and in its own way was a "healing" came through Arthur Ford [the well known medium who passed on several years ago]. This took place about ten years ago in Chicago, where the President of our Church, Fred Hoskins, who had shortly before passed over, came through Arthur. At that point I was a little discouraged at some of the parishional limitations I encountered. First, Hoskins came through, by means of Ford's mediumship, with some very evidential material. And then he added a message which was a very beautiful one and has helped me many times. Fred Hoskins said that the Holy Spirit is working on "this side," as well as on "that side." He urged me not to be discouraged. He said this: "The Church Visible and the Church Invisible constitutes the Church Indivisible." Just those few words had tremendous impact on me, then and there.

EBON: That, of course, was both very poetic and very strong.

BATZLER: Exactly. I have used this phrase very often since then, both for myself and others who were going through a difficult period. That is one of the most specific instances of a healing effect from the other side.

EBON: Was it, like in welding, when a little bit of molten lead brings two wires together and establishes a complete circuit?

BATZLER: Yes. And from this I moved on, from the element of survival that was instrumental in creating a healing effect, toward the point where I began to regard survival after death as a condition on its own. This started to take place about 1967. It was in the context of the activities of Spiritual Frontiers Fellowship, including my work with Arthur Ford and the Worralls. This became very meaningful to me, and it is one reason why I have the commitment to SFF that I do.

EBON: Leaving aside what I call the circumstantial evidence for life after death, the scientific or pseudo scientific paraphernalia, what is your very personal conviction on after life right now?

BATZLER: My conviction is based on an accumulation of factors. First, there is my study of the history of man in terms of his religious quest, especially the quest for eternal life. This also includes the philosophers' "proofs" for this extension of life. Also, my study of both the Old and New Testament has made me more sensitive to the whole question of Survival and Resurrection. Realizing that Resurrection, for the Christian faith, is essential, I am very conscious of the fact that—at least in contemporary theology—there is very little discussion of this central aspect of our tradition. The whole area of parapsychology has added to my knowledge. My existential understanding of this subject has been mainly through my own work with the dying, as a pastor, and that has made it all a lot more real for me.

EBON: How do you link these theoretical and practical aspects with each other?

BATZLER: I have seen people move from one condition to another, through various stages of despair; and, of course, beyond despair. I seek to link the concept of the Resurrection and the New Testament witness with the experience of human death and the concrete hopes and affirmations of individuals who are near death and are willing to talk about resurrection.

EBON: How many people have you seen dying?

BATZLER: Let me consider this in the various stages that dying represents. I have seen perhaps as many as two hundred people during various terminal period and some forty to fifty at or very near, the instant of death.

EBON: Have these actual deathbed impressions strengthened your personal belief?

BATZLER: Yes, certainly. But only just recently. I've still got a long way to go. I am still trying to be more aware of and sensitive to this kind of convincing experience so that I can better minister to the people who really need it.

EBON: Does that mean, if I may put it crudely, that you find yourself thinking, "Well, I sure hope that what I'm telling them is true!" Doesn't that create a problem?

BATZLER: It does and it still is a problem for me. And that's one of the reasons for my intense interest for work in this field. I don't expect to solve the problem in any ultimate sense, but I do want to be more effective in my work. I also want to share these insights with my colleagues.

EBON: It just occurs to me that I haven't asked you the one and crucial question: Do you believe in life after death?

BATZLER: I do.

EBON: Is it a matter of faith, rather than of being convinced by scientific evidence?

BATZLER: Primarily, I'd say, yes.

EBON: Do we actually need to have our faith in life after

death documented and supported by evidence accumulated, so to speak, in the laboratory?

BATZLER: From where I stand today, I'd say, No.

EBON: But then, what are you looking for, and where are you looking?

BATZLER: I am looking for a deeper understanding and expressing of my faith. That means I am constantly going back to the New Testament. But I am also looking at other faiths. I want to know what other religions are saying about life after death, about immortality or the Resurrection. I do not expect this quest ever to end. It is in this questing that I believe more truth will be unveiled.

15. The Living Instruments

Douglas Johnson is an erudite, soft-spoken Englishman, who served in the Royal Air Force during World War Two and then became one of the world's best-known mediums. In contrast to many other human links to the spirit world, his name has never been associated with rumors of possible fraud—not even the slightest suggestion of it. Johnson accepted his gift with reluctance, even fear. But that is another part of his story, and not the reason I'm starting this chapter with this brief profile of the man; he not only is a channel for entities from "the other side," but he also hears and sees them while he is not in trance.

And that can be awkward. Particularly if you can't tell whether you are seeing someone who is alive or dead.

One evening, Johnson was sitting in a London bar with a friend, drinking a glass of sherry and talking quietly. They were at a table but could see the bar itself, which was just a few feet way. Over there, standing at the bar was a black man, a West Indian, and next to him an older woman wearing the native dress of what could have been a village in Jamaica, Trinidad or one of the other islands of the former British possessions in the West Indies, in the Caribbean. There are now several hundreds of thousands of West Indians in England, but nearly all of them wear European clothes. The woman's get-up puzzled Johnson, and he said to his friend, "Isn't that strange—look at that woman in native dress."

The friend looked to the bar and replied, puzzled, "I don't see her. I can see a West Indian in an ordinary suit and sport jacket." Knowing Douglas Johnson and his propensity for spirits, he added, "She must be one of your spooks. You'd better get down and talk to her."

As Johnson recalled the encounter later, he went to the bar all right, but the woman had disappeared. Trying to get his bearings on this odd encounter, he invited the West Indian to take his drink to their table and join the two. The man looked surprised, but agreed. As soon as he had sat down, the woman reappeared. Her voice sort of dropped into Johnson's mind, "This is my son. He is going to do something foolish tonight. Stop him!"

Consorting with spirits is one thing, telling strangers about it, another. Johnson figured that, at worst, the black man could regard him as crazy; and, at best, something good could come out of their meeting. So he said, "Your mother just told me that you're going to do something very foolish tonight—and you're not to do it."

The man seemed shocked and replied, "It could not be my other. She is dead."

But the voice in Johnson's mind now said, "Tell him that I was blind from birth, and that I can see again in the spirit world."

This seemed to convince the young man that there was something genuine and important going on. Obviously shaken, he said, "This must be mother—tell her I won't do it."

The three men became quite friendly after that. The West Indian eventually told Johnson that he had planned to act as lookout during a bank robbery that evening. When they met again, a week or so later, he reported that all others who had participated in the robbery had been caught, while he, warned by his mother, had stayed away from the caper.

Johnson told this story in an interview with the magazine *Psychic* (February 1971) and said that he regarded the incident as "direct intervention from the next world, from a mother who loves her son and is anxious to protect him from harm." The reader of this book knows, by now, that scientists can nearly always come up with an alternate explanation, and I'll give one here just to show that it is possible even in what seems such a strong, clear-cut case. Douglas Johnson is gifted with telepathic ability, and what he picked up when he looked over at the bar may have been the subconscious worry of the young West Indian, perhaps even his conflict with an upbringing at home, under his mother's strong discipline, her sense of right and wrong. Later, Johnson also picked up not only the visual image of the man's memory of his mother, but also the fact that she had been born blind. Mixed with Johnson's own ideas on a spirit world beyond death, the man's conflict became dramatized into an auditory impression, the woman's voice, in addition to the visual impression of her person, dressed in native clothes.

Somehow, this telepathy explanation is fancier and less convincing than Johnson's own, which carries with it the emotional element of a mother's worry about her son, at a crucial moment of his life, a concern beyond death. The British medium is well aware of the delicate position in which a human instrument, who links the living with the dead, often finds himself. His own path into mediumship illustrates this point. Although it began, as is often the case with mediums, early in life, he was frightened by it. When he was about six years old, he would tell his mother, "Granny is coming to lunch today." And although the mother said, "Nonsense," his grandmother would turn up. It had been a case of good, old-fashioned telepathy between grandmother and grandchild, supplementing the emotional link that often holds these two separate generations together.

Johnson remembers that he attended sittings with other mediums when he was a young man. Once he visited the British College of Psychic Science in London and had a séance with Eileen Garrett. Johnson told *Psychic* that "it was about four o'clock on a winter afternoon and was getting dusk. I was asked to sit down and Mrs. Garrett went into trance. It was a very remarkable trance. My mother appeared to communicate extremely well—I was called by my pet name and there were many other extremely evidential facts given. By the time the sitting ended the room was dark. When Mrs. Garrett came out of her trance state and turned around to switch on the light by her side, she suddenly looked at me very surprised and said, 'You're much too young to waste money on me. You should be spending it on beer and girls.' So I told her she was my birthday present from an aunt."

Douglas Johnson's scare came when he was fifteen years old. He had been taken to a psychic development class and was sitting in a small, stuffy room with a group of people. He felt woozy, but didn't want to break up the mediumistic circle, in which everyone was holding hands, and hoped the feeling would pass. Next thing he knew, his host handed him a glass of water. Three quarters of an hour had passed, Johnson had been in a mediumistic trance, and someone had been speaking through him: a Chinese who called himself "Chiang."

The idea of just passing out, losing control of yourself, and some Oriental stranger turning you into something like a ventriloquist's dummy, very much upset young Douglas. He feared he might slip into a faint-like trance under awkward circumstances, such as on a bus or in school. Once this fear subsided, he did go into trances, and continued this method until he was twenty years old. While in the air force, the College of Psychic Science used to let him use their library by mail. After the war, in 1947, Douglas Johnson began to give sittings for others on a fairly regular basis.

Today, Johnson is a professional medium in England and during visits to the United States. A number of American parapsychologists have found him a helpful and cooperative subject in their experiments. The whole business of a medium's having a Spirit Control is an odd, but persistent phenomenon. The control usually acts as a "guide" or master of ceremonies who makes sure that the medium is protected, or as a traffic cop who keeps control over the comings and goings of spirits during a séance. The medium who was the subject of an extended study by the noted philosopher-psychologist, William James, was Mrs. Leonore Piper, and she had a control called "Phinuit." A noted British medium, Mrs. Gladys Osborne Leonard, had as her control a young woman, "Feda." When I used to visit Frank Decker in New York, the voice of a young boy, "Patsy," could be heard as that of the spirit control. Eileen Garrett had "Uvani" as the "gatekeeper" who usually put in only a short appearance at the beginning of a sitting, and "Abdul Latif" as the less laconic and more cordial "guide.' Arthur Ford's control was "Fletcher," a man he had known when he was alive. The editor of London's Spiritualist weekly, *Psychic News*, the highly professional Maurice Barbanell, occasionally becomes a human link between the two worlds (*Two Worlds* is also the title of another publication he edits) and has a control called "Silver Birch," an American Indian.

The editors of *Psychic* asked Johnson what he thought of the fact that so many guides are "exotic Eastern types," and he answered: "Well, the skeptic would say that they are more dramatic. But it may be that North American Indians, the ancient Egyptians, the Chinese and so on, were brought up with a belief in communication with the next world. And therefore, when they go to the next world, they would have knowledge that would make it easier for them to control the necessary forces for communication. But I have to say that I do not know. I do know people who have European guides. Too, I think guides are often higher aspects of someone. They often appear to have a greater sense of wisdom and understanding than the person they come through. Therefore, they are helpful, and I think one should accept them as that, though not as all-knowledgeable."

The idea that guides are "higher aspects" of a medium opens the door to an interpretation of spirit communications that is in line with psychological speculation on the nature of mediumship generally. Simply put, this means that mediums use their role to express ambitions or creative potentials that, for some reason, they are reluctant to expose in their own name and as part of their very own personalities. This is akin to a novelist who may be a mousy, introvert creature but creates characters who are adventurist, highly sexed and eminently extravert. Some actors or actresses are colorless persons in their own right, but can give dramatic expression to a character created by a playwright.

We have similar phenomena in the history of religion. Prophets of nearly every faith usually declaim that they are not speaking for themselves, but that God is manifesting through them. When people say they are "inspired," they forget that the original meaning of the word is that they are "filled with a spirit," usually thought of as divine. St. John, who wrote the last Book of the New Testament, "Revelation," said that he was "in the spirit" and suggested that either God or Christ were in effect conveying their messages through him.

The phrase, "I am only an instrument" is very frequently used by practitioners of some psychic or pseudo-psychic gift. One of these is the Washington seeress, Mrs. Jeane Dixon, who maintains that she is simply acting, as it were, as the Divinity's transmission belt. But what about people who display actual creative talent only when, as they believe, they are acting as human links between discarnate spirits and the rest of us?

Let me cite the two most striking examples, one in literature, the other in music. The first is the story of a St. Louis housewife, Mrs. Pearl Lenore Curran, through whom an entity who called herself Patience Worth communicated a stream of writings couched in terms of the seventeenth century; the other is the British musician-medium Rosemary Brown, who plays what she describes as "new" compositions by some of the world's outstanding dead composers.

The Patience Worth story began in 1913, when Mrs. Curran first received a message on a Ouija board, which said, "Many moons ago I lived. Again I come. Patience Worth is my name." It continued, "Wait I would speak with thee. If thought shalt live, then so shall I. I make my bread by thy hearth. Good friends, let us be merrie. The time for work is past. Let the tabbie drowse and blink her wisdom by the firelog."

With Mrs. Curran, wife of a the former Immigration Commissioner of Missouri, John H. Curran, was her friend Mrs. Emily Grant Hutchings, wife of the Secretary of the Tower Grove Park Board of St. Louis. I shall give some highlights of this case of a "human link" with the world beyond death, which remains the best illustration of literature being created in this manner. Three books have been written on this remarkable case. The first, by Casper S. Yost, was *Patience Worth: A Psychic Mystery* (New York, 1916); the second by Walter Franklin Prince, *The Case of Patience Worth* (Boston, 1927); the third, and so far the definitive one, by Irving Litvag, *Singer in the Shadows: The Strange Case of Patience Worth* (New York, 1972).

Yost said that on that July evening in St. Louis, a series of communications began that "in intellectual vigor and literary quality are virtually without precedent in the scant imaginative literature quoted in the chronicles of psychic phenomena. The personality of Patience Worth—if Personality it may be called—so impressed itself upon these women, at the first visit, that they got pencil and paper and put down not only all that she transmitted through the board, but all the questions and comments that elicited her remarks; and at every meeting since then, a verbatim record has been made of the conversations, and the communications."

Yost listed the communications as including "conversations, maxims, epigrams, allegories, tales, dramas, poems, all the way from sportive to religious, and even prayers, most of them of no little beauty and of a character that may reasonably be considered unique in literature." According to Litvag's count, the Patience Worth writings now in the archives of the Missouri Historical Society fill twenty-nine bound volumes, totaling 4,375 single-spaced pages.

At first, the writings of Patience Worth attracted wide interest. Yost's book found a receptive audience. But the intricate style and extraordinary length of some of the Patience Worth writings limited their readability. Literary scholars were difficult to convince that her language was authentic. Among her major efforts was *The Sorry Tale*, a long historical novel set at the time of Christ, which took nearly two years to complete. Part of the effort to introduce her work into the literary marketplace was a visit by the Currans to New York, where they visited the publisher Henry Holt and his associate, Alfred Harcourt; the names of both men are prominent in two major book publishing firms today; Holt, Rinehart & Winston, and Harcourt Brace Jovanovich. At various times, Holt and Harcourt placed their hands on the talking board with Mrs. Curran, while segments of *The Sorry Tale* were dictated by Patience Worth.

When Harcourt took over from Holt, Patience was asked whether she was aware of the change. Here, in her characteristic style, is the reply:

"Yea. Here be one who holdeth o' the grams. Yea he holdeth athin his hand worth and doth to set him up then a pot 'o brew and set ahotted till the brew doth smell it at afinished and areadied for the eat o' hungered. Then doth he to taste thereof and wag him 'yea' and 'nea.' "

Litvag observed that this comment provided a startlingly accurate portrayal of "Harcourt's work in evaluating manuscripts and his custom of preparing and sipping a hot beverage as he made his editorial decisions." Mrs. Curran, he noted, "as far as they knew, had no way of knowing these things about Harcourt's duties and work habits." The two publishing executives proceeded to discuss jacket design and other production details with Patience Worth. When Harcourt asked whether Mrs. Curran's picture should be used, Patience answered, "Think ye that I be awish o' flesh? She be but the pot."

Was Pearl Curran only the "pot" into which Patience Worth poured her literary output, to be emptied into the bowls of a general public?

After all these years, no one can tell for sure. If, as in the little scene with Harcourt, Mrs. Curran was practicing telepathy and putting her impressions into Patience's language, some sort of explanation that eliminates the spirit as a real entity can be devised. But the very speed, ease and facility with which the writings were done seems to have exceeded even above-average human skill. Patience could produce poems on order, even when asked to start each line with a different letter of the alphabet, excepting "X." She could dictate segments separately and then fit them together into an orderly whole. The question continued to be asked: if Mrs. Curran had the skill to write the Patience Worth material, why didn't she do so under her own name, and not have to face the doubt and criticism that her "spirit writing" aroused? We don't know enough about her possibly sublimated ambitions and skills as a writer, although Litvak refers to a short story she sold to the *Saturday Evening Post* on her own, and which featured a secondary personality created by a woman who exclaimed, "Well, I just didn't want to be me. I was sick of myself. I wanted to feel, feel like a woman that somebody cared about . . ."

Probably the closest contemporary parallel to Patience Worth is "Seth," the entity associated with Ms. Jane Roberts. These communications began in 1963, and the pattern follows that of Patience Worth and other automatic writings in that it moved from the talking board to a point where Mrs. Roberts "heard" whole sentences in her mind, before they were spelled out on the board. The comparison ends right there, because Jane Roberts goes into trances, which Mrs. Curran never did; and Seth espouses religio-philosophical and psychic ideas, whereas the Patience Worth texts were mainly fiction and poetry, although Patience commented freely on abstract subjects as well.

In such works as *The Seth Material* (Englewood Cliffs, N.J., 1970) and several later books, Seth speaks extensively on reincarnation and other popular psychic subjects. Mrs. Roberts, unlike Mrs. Curran, had published poetry and nonfiction before the appearance of the Seth entity in her life. Two of her novels are *The Rebellers* and *Bundu*, and among her non-fiction is *How to Develop Your ESP Power*. I think that many readers of the Seth texts do so on the assumption that he is a discarnate entity, a "spirit," pure and simple. But Jane Roberts deals with the question of identity in sophisticated terms, as when she asks "Who or What is Seth?" In answer, Mrs. Roberts says she "avoided calling Seth a spirit and leaving it at that." She doesn't like the phrase, "spirit," and thinks it would be "too easy an answer." She adds:

"In accepting one solution, we may be closing our minds to others that lie beneath. I am not saying that Seth is *just* a psychological structure allowing me to tune into revelational knowledge, nor denying that he has an independent existence. I do think that some kind of blending must take place in sessions between his personality and mine, and that this 'psychological bridge' *itself* is a legitimate structure that must take place in any such communication. Seth is at his end, and I am at mine. I agree with Seth here. I don't think it is a relatively simple matter of a medium just blacking out and acting like a telephone connection. I do think that Seth is part of another entity, and that he is something quite different from, say a friend who has 'survived' death."

These are complex ideas. But, if we want to be honest with ourselves, we've got to keep our minds open to them all. It is well and good that the people who have been over the clinical edge into death tell us of their new confidence in an afterlife; it is soothing to the bereaved to go to a séance and find themselves, in intimate terms, addressed by their beloved; it is fascinating to assume that someone like Patience Worth actually communicated a whole body of literature through the "human link" provided by a living person. But we are obviously dealing with a frontier that must be approached from many directions, and the evidence and opinions we have on hand suggest that we do not exclude any particular mode of after-life existence.

And now to the woman who has claimed that she receives post-mortem compositions from some of the world's greatest composers. She is, as I said before, Rosemary Brown. She lives in England, but has visited the United States to talk about her experiences and to perform some of the compositions on the piano. When Mrs. Brown gave a concert in New York's Town Hall, I was one of the panel of experts who had been called upon to evaluate the significance of Rosemary Brown's claims.

It was a delightful evening, sponsored by the New York Area group of Spiritual Frontiers Fellowship, a nation-wide organization devoted to exploring interrelationships between religion and psychic phenomena. Mrs. Brown is a modest, middle-aged Englishwoman who presents herself as a typical surburban housewife who finds herself at the receiving end of messages and "new" compositions by such luminaries as Franz Liszt; Liszt's role with her is very much in the nature of the guide or Spirit Control in other mediums. "All of the composers who have been to see me have, in the first instance, arrived accompanied by Liszt," she says.

In her book, *Unfinished Symphonies* (New York, 1971), Mrs. Brown speaks of her special relationship with Liszt and says that he introduced the other composers to her, because "he is the organizer of this group of musicians who have been using me to work with them." Even after the other composers "come on their own," Liszt is "generally there somewhere in the background, watching to see how things go."

Rosemary Brown's experiences follow a pattern that can be found in many mediums, beginning very early in life. She first "saw" Liszt when she was only seven years old, but was "already accustomed to seeing the spirits of the socalled dead." As she recalls the figure of the composer's ghost, a white-haired old man, he said, "When you grow up I will come back and give you music." Little Rosemary was so "used to seeing people from another world" that she didn't think much of their appearance, and she didn't mention Liszt's visit to her. The composer did return, became "the organizer and leader of a group of famous composers who visit me at my home and give me their new compositions." By 1970, Mrs. Brown had accumulated 400 pieces of music in this way.

Among the work developed during the first six years of her contact with the composers were "songs, piano pieces, some incomplete string quartets, the beginning of an opera as well as partly completed concertos and symphonies." Records have been made of her spirit compositions. Just like Douglas Johnson, Eileen Garrett and other mediums, Mrs. Brown had upset her mother when she was still young, telling her things that she "couldn't possibly know," because they had happened "before you were born."

Today, Mrs. Brown feels pleased that she, rather than some distinguished composer or musician, has been selected to receive these compositions, but she admits that it has caused problems. In her book, *Unfinished Symphonies*, she says: "The work I do is fascinating and I have dedicated myself to be the intermediary to the best of my ability, but because of the closed minds of the world there are times when I wish perhaps that someone else had been chosen for the task."

At any rate, the New York audience to whom she talked and played was most cordial and receptive. Plainly dressed, Rosemary Brown projected a mixture of humble pride and sincere puzzlement about it all. She described her simple life, her widowhood, the need to work five hours a day at a school meals service to make ends meet. She continued, in the same unassuming fashion, to talk about her encounters with Beethoven, Schubert, Chopin, Rachmaninoff and Brahms (she found Brahms rather stern and forbidding, a tough master).

And then she played. As a matter of fact, she played quite expertly and with practiced ease. Musicologists are as mixed in their analyses of Mrs. Brown's spirit compositions as experts are on just about every subject under the sun. Some have called these works "imitative," others "startingly genuine." I, as a non-musicologist, contributed to the panel's opinions the overall view that similar cases of mediumistic creativity permit. Mrs. Brown is a Mrs. Curran of the piano, just as Mrs. Curran was a Mrs. Brown of the pen. Both, I assume, had creative potentials that existed before they received any impulses from the spirit world; it has been easier for them to express these impulses under other labels. And yet, the workings of creativity are themselves inextricably linked to that elusive quality we call "inspiration," and its source remains a mystery. Both women became "human links" with another world, be it a World of the Spirit or a World of Creativity.

A relative newcomer to the field is the young British psychic Matthew Manning, an extraordinarily versatile person who has contributed a third dimension to psychic creativity: he draws in the style of discarnate painters of the past, much as Mrs. Brown writes down compositions. Among automatic drawings by Manning are examples of the work by Albrecht Dürer, executed in that master's characteristic meticulous detail, and by Pablo Picasso, the wide-ranging Spanish painter. In my book *What's New in ESP?*, which contained a chapter on Manning's past and present phenomena, I said that his drawings are variously "interpreted as clairvoyant replicas of existing works of art, as spirit drawings, or as elaborations of his own unconscious." This psychic has also been able to make "diagnoses" seemingly communicated through him by a discarnate medical man, "Thomas Penn." Diagnoses and even treatment under the apparent direction of spirit doctors is an inter-cultural phenomenon ranging from Britain to Brazil, and to be found in many different parts of the globe.

Mediums who function as human links between another dimension, or spirit world, and our own level of consciousness operate, as we have seen, on such creative levels as literature, music and art. Spirit healing can be found for the most part in societies where the danger of legal action for "practicing medicine without a license" does not exist. How, and even why, certain human links are chosen to express such gifts is, for all practical purposes, totally unknown. But even before we can answer this question, another arises: can we dispense with human links and, by the use of special machinery, construct nonhuman links with the world beyond?

The subject of what is technically known as "apparatus communication with discarnate persons" has been explored tenaciously by a former RCA engineer, Mr. Julius Weinberger. In experimenting with a variety of "sensitive" intermediaries between the living and the dead, Weinberger worked for some four years with a plant, the Venus Flytrap (*Dionaea muscipula*), and reports that it has shown responses that might make it "applicable to investigations involving contact with discarnate persons." No purely non-biological intermediary has, as yet, shown similar degrees of sensitivity and research potential.

16. Did Houdini Return
from the Dead?

In the introductory chapter to this book, I described my puzzlement at encountering, at the first séance I ever attended, the alleged spirit of Dr. Walter Franklin Prince, research director of the American Society for Psychical Research, who told me about his errors in doubting the reliability of the Boston medium, Margery Crandon. Another such incident had taken place earlier, when the spirit of the great magician and medium debunker, Harry Houdini, confirmed his after-death existence and wished to atone for wrong-doings against Mrs. Crandon.

All this must be taken with many grains of salt. I rather doubt that the late Dr. Prince, whom I now greatly admire as a tolerant but skeptical investigator, singled out a very young and ignorant Martin Ebon to talk rather weepily, as I recall, about his errors while "on this side." The Houdini séance is equally open to doubt. The magician had used a code during performances, which was only known to his wife, Beatric.

Eventually, the code was mentioned in a séance given by Arthur Ford on January 7, 1929. It consisted of a ten-word message that made up the line, "Rosabelle—Answer—Tell—Pray—Answer—Look—Tell—Answer—Answer—Tell." Mrs. Houdini wrote a letter shortly afterward, testifying that this had, in fact, been the code that she and her husband used. Later still, she denied that this post-mortem message had been genuine and suggested that Ford had obtained the information by other means. Later still, and following Arthur Ford's death, evidence that he had actually used fradulent methods, at least on occasion (notably, a Toronto séance given for the late Bishop James A. Pike, for which he appeared to have prepared himself with information gathered from the obituary pages of *The New York Times*). In addition, gossip in magicians' circles suggested that Ford and Houdini's widow had, for a time, been friendly enough for her to have given him the code herself.

With all that in mind, and to illustrate how elusive and convoluted "proof" of survival after death through mediumistic channels can be, I want to introduce the reader to the work of Carl Wickland, MD., who was a practicing psychiatrist in Chicago and Los Angeles in the 1920s and 1930s. He acted on the assumption that certain forms of mental illness are due to spirit possession. He used light electric shock to oust the spirit from his patient and had it talk through his wife, Anna, a medium. Then, by a mixture of enlightenment and threats, Wickland would seem to convince the misplaced entity to leave the body of the patient and go on to more advanced spirit realms. In this book *The Gateway to Understanding* Dr. Wickland describes a séance he held at the home of Sir Arthur Conan Doyle, creator of the fictional detective Sherlock Holmes and a devoted spiritualist. This happened after Houdini's death and the "revelation" of his code through Ford's medium-ship. In his lifetime, Houdini had feuded with Conan Doyle privately and publicly. The two prominent men, the popular author and the still more popular magician, appeared on lecture platforms and debated the issue of life after death extensively and stridently. Houdini tried to show Conan Doyle that he could duplicate all mediumistic communications by trickery, and had achieved remarkable skills in doing just that. But he never succeeded in convincing Doyle that spirits did not speak through mediums.

At any rate, the séance arranged by Dr. Wickland had his wife act as a medium. As Wickland described it, "among other intelligences the spirit of Harry Houdini, the great magician, took control of Mrs. Wickland. At the outset the Houdini spirit "complained bitterly of his dark surroundings and referred to the great mistake he had made in ridiculing psychic phenomena, which he knew to be true." Wickland's account continues:

"Asked about the code agreed upon between himself and his wife, he declared that in his present mental confusion he could not even recall what the code was, and that he must first acquire more understanding of his new condition, for he had a very great deal to learn and undo." Wickland added:

"At the time, I was rather surprised regarding his seeming familiarity with Sir Arthur, but learned later that Houdini, while in life, had had many discussions with Sir Arthur anent the problem of spirit return, and also that Houdini had expressed a leaning toward the reality of spirit communication. Readers are familiar with the recent successful decoding, through the mediumship of Mr. Arthur Ford of New York of Houdini's secret code agreed upon between his wife and himself, at the time acknowledged by affidavit of Mrs. Houdini to be authentic."

Wickland added that "three years later, during a private séance at our home, the spirit of Houdini again controlled Mrs. Wickland, expressed "great regret at the stand he had taken while on earth against the truth of spirit return and communication, and declared he was now trying to do all within his power to right the wrong." Wickland quoted Houdini as follows:

"It seems cruel that a man in my position should have thrown dust in the eyes of people as I did. Since my passing I have gone to many, many mediums but the door is closed to me. When I was on earth I closed the door with double locks by ridiculing psychic phenomena and mediums. I have been able to open the door once or twice, but only for a little while. When I try to tell people of the real truth they say I am not the one I claim to be, because when I was on earth I did not talk that way."

"I ask you here to give me good thoughts, strength and power to undo my mistakes. I cannot progress until I have acknowledged the truth. I must, I must do it! I found an avenue through that most wonderful medium, Arthur Ford, and gave my wife the code we had agreed upon. I have done great harm to many mediums. How I wish I could go to every one and tell them that I did a wrong thing, that when they worked for the good of the cause I tried to expose them to the world as humbugs. God help me for having done that. I see my mistakes but I cannot get out of my present condition until I do good to the ones I ridiculed. I try my best to correct my mistakes but it is very hard."

Whatever the merit or validity of these communications recorded by Dr. Wickland, their tenor and manner were certainly unlike those displayed by Houdini while among the living "on this side." The confusion, veritable whimpering and contriteness remind me of the "talk" I had with the alleged spirit of Dr. Prince, and I find them equally puzzling and trite. The Houdini-Wickland conversation, as recorded by Dr. Wickland, is reproduced below (I have substituted "Wickland" for the abbreviation "Dr.", as given in the book, and "Houdini" for "Sp.", an abbreviation for "Spirit"):

WICKLAND: Do you recall the talk you had with Sir Arthur Conan Doyle shortly after you passed out? You spoke then through this same instrument.

HOUDINI: I tried my best to get through the opening but at that time I was so bewildered I did not know where I was. In my own soul I am so convinced of the wrongs I committed. Many do not know what awaits them on the other side of life, what the sleep of death is. When one has an understanding of death, there is no waiting, no hindrance. At first I was so confused that everything which belonged to memory was forgotten for quite a long time. (A common complaint of many spirits in their first efforts to communicate after transition.) Later, things came clearly to me, the things I had promised to do, and I tried very hard to get a message through. I wanted to tell the truth and undo my former error. I found a wonderful instrument in Mr. Ford. I talked through him and my wife was in a receptive spirit to accept me. I was very happy but suddenly the door was shut.

How I also wish I could say a few words to another very wonderful medium, Margery. (Mrs. Crandon, of Boston.) I did much harm to that poor woman. How she has suffered because of my antagonistic thoughts. I tried to upset her and once I nearly killed her, but I did not think much of it at the time. I wish I could undo the wrong I did her. She is a very wonderful medium. I lectured and charged money—for what? To blind the eyes of the people. They would pay to hear me lecture and run down poor, honest mediums. (Covering face with hands.) Oh, it is awful.

WICKLAND: Do not carry on that way, friend. You are controlling a medium and must be more careful. Do not over-excite yourself.

HOUDINI: I see things so differently now. Everything I did stands out before me.

WICKLAND: Change your attitude and look for the intelligent spirits around you. Do not think of your troubles all the time. Work your way out of them.

HOUDINI: But it is as if I am in a prison and cannot see anything.

WICKLAND: You will see in time. Ask the intelligent forces to give you strength and power to overcome so you can carry on.

HOUDINI: (Features brightening.) Thank you! I can see more clearly now. Standing here is a very beautiful little lady (spirit) and she says she will help me. (To spirit.) You say you will take me to your home?

WICKLAND: Does she say who she is?

HOUDINI: (Addressing an invisible.) What is your name, pretty little lady? She says her name is Miss Dresser. (Former member of our circle.) And you say you will take me and help me? I knew better in my heart than to lecture as I did. I did it, however, for money, money! I was so selfish.

WICKLAND: You can overcome that.

HOUDINI: Beautiful lady, will you really help me? How peaceful your soul must be. You are like a transparent angel!

WICKLAND: Her mind was occupied with higher ideals while in the physical body.

HOUDINI: She seems to float, not walk, and here I am, as heavy as lead.

WICKLAND: You must not think of that all the time. You made mistakes, but from now on determine to see the better side. Do not be so discouraged.

HOUDINI: You will give me your help, little lady?

WICKLAND: Of course she will. That is why she came here tonight. Until recently, she met with us in this little circle.

HOUDINI: Will you all send thoughts to me for strength? I know I did wrong, and I knew I was wrong at the time. If I had done what my conscience urged me to do, I would not be where I am now. I was a psychic, and I knew it. I was helped in my work by the spirit forces, but more by the materially-minded forces, those who could work magic. But I shut the door to the higher intelligences.

Little lady, you who are so beautiful and bright, will you help me? Another one comes to me now. Listen! Listen to that beautiful music! This little lady has brought two others who are now singing. Such music! At last my soul is at peace and I can go on. I have much work to do to right the wrongs of my past. But listen, such beautiful music! Heaven is opening! I cannot describe this music because I never heard anything like it before. And see those most beautiful flowers! Never, never, have I seen such beauty. Heaven is surely opening for me!

WICKLAND: You will find many wonderful things in your new life but you will have to work your way out of your present condition. Realize your mistakes and profit by them. Life is a school.

HOUDINI: Can you hear that wonderful orchestra playing? They tell me it is an orchestra that plays to open the eyes of those in darkness so they can see the beauty of the spirit world. Oh, how I do wish I could tell my wife that I can see! It would make her so happy to know that I have found peace.

WICKLAND: We will all send you helpful thoughts.

HOUDINI: One thing I must ask all of you, and that is, do not be doubting Thomases as to my identity. I have enough to combat now. I *am* Houdini. What place is this?

WICKLAND: This is The National Psychological Institute in Los Angeles, established for research in normal and abnormal psychology to ascertain the condition of spirits after transition. Experience has shown that intelligent spirits play an important role for good in human affairs; on the other hand, many spirits, owing to ignorance, often unwittingly act as contributing factors in many mental aberrations. This is also a clearing-house where intelligent spirits, in co-operation with mortals, can enlighten the perplexed spirits who are often unaware of their transition.

HOUDINI: Now they tell me I must leave. But before going I want to thank you for the help I have received. God bless you all! Good-bye.

Wickland states that a report of this communication from Houdini "was published in an eastern magazine and ten days later the spirit of Houdini again controlled Mrs. Wickland." Their exchange follows:

HOUDINI: I have come to thank you for the help you have given me.

WICKLAND: Did we help you much?

HOUDINI: Yes, and I am much happier now. I had denied facts which I knew in my heart were true. I wanted to be original and have everybody think I was scientific, so I denied facts and criticised others. When you have the truth, acknowledge it. Now I have acknowledged my mistakes and I want to ask forgiveness of the ones I tried to harm. I thank you for publishing that article and letting the public know that I came back. I am glad it was given out to the world that I confessed I wanted to ruin that little medium, Margery (Mrs. Crandon) who lives only for the truth and sacrifices her life to demonstrate her work. I tried trickery with her but Walter (Mrs. Crandon's spirit brother) found me out beforehand. God bless the Crandons and God bless you! I am so glad that article was given out to show that poor Mrs. Crandon was persecuted. That is now known.

WICKLAND: Many believed that you were a wonderful medium yourself and that spirits helped you in your work. Was that correct?

HOUDINI: Yes, but I would not acknowledge it. Whenever I was going to do something spectacular, if I did not hear a voice telling me to go ahead I did not dare to go on. Many times I did not perform my tricks because I did not hear the voice. When I heard it I knew that everything was all right. I cannot tell you exactly how I did my tricks because I do not know myself. I was in a semitrance when all that took place.

WICKLAND: I should like to know who got you out of the tank of water and came up on the stage from the front. I claim that could not have been done without spirit agencies.

HOUDINI: I do not even know myself how it was done. When I was in the tank of water I could hear the voices talking but I could not hear what was said. Up to a certain point I was myself, but not after that. From the time I was tied and locked up until I was free I did not know what took place. But I could not have told that. People would have wondered what was the matter with me and that is the reason I did not dare say anything. I wanted them to think I was doing the tricks myself, but the spirits were the ones who acted through me.

WICKLAND: You are making progress now, are you not?

HOUDINI: Yes; I have progressed far enough to give enlightenment to some and I do all I can to help the unfortunate ones. I have certain duties to do to help others before I can progress to new development. I am happy but in a way I am restricted because I have to find those who are in trouble and help them and give them strength. I do work now that I should have done in earth life. If I had stood for the truth and given credit to spirit power, the world would have been more enlightened, because the spirits did wonderful things through me.

WICKLAND: Have you contacted the spirit of Sir Arthur? (Sir Arthur Conan Doyle.)

HOUDINI: Yes, and I have also asked him to forgive me. I said many unkind things about him. I was down on all Psychic Research and on every good medium. If I had happened to know you, Dr. Wickland, and your wife, you would also have gotten something. Those who escaped only did so because they had not come under my notice. I thought I knew it all and that there was nothing more to learn. I want to tell you, whenever you reach that state of mind where you know it all, ask God to help you out of it. When you feel you know everything and condemn everybody and have the idea that you are the only one, it is very bad. There is always something to learn. The more you learn the better it is for you. I am more than glad that the world knows I came back and have asked to be forgiven. That means more to me than I can explain. I thank you for the light you gave me. Now I will not take up any more of your time, but I thank all of you.

WICKLAND: We all wish you well.

HOUDINI: Thank you and Good-night.

This exchange between Dr. Wickland and the supposed spirit of Harry Houdini, through the mediumship of Anna Wickland, followed a pattern typical of Wickland's attitude and procedure. Most of the time, Carl Wickland addressed entities communicating through his wife in the manner of an erudite physician-psychiatrist who seeks to enlighten a not-very-well-informed patient or benighted truth-seeker. Wickland could on occasion be supportive, educational and patient; at other times he appeared to be brow-beating and threatening a spirit, particularly when he was dealing with what seemed to him an entity set on possessing a man or woman who, to others, might appear to be emotionally disturbed.

In the case of Houdini, possession, and therefore exorcism by the Wickland method, was not involved. Wickland was concerned with "verification of spirit identity." His discussion with the Houdini entity supplied, as he saw it, evidence of the magician's after-death identity. Other researchers, then and now, would conclude that Mrs. Wickland's unconscious was providing her husband with the kind of communication he required; the "Houdini spirit" in this exchange did not provide

actual evidence of identity, or anything outside the range of
Wickland's dogma of spirit existences.

It is nevertheless quite possible that Dr. Wickland's unique
and tightly structured psychiatric treatment method—if it
may be classified as such—did help patients who shared his
views, or came to share them, concerning spirit existence,
possession, and exorcism by electrical shock, plus Wickland's
single-minded "education" of the spirits. He maintained that
his treatment was suggested to him by high-level spirit entities, and that he was merely cooperating with them. At the
end of the Houdini dialogue, Wickland stated that "Intelligent Spirit Forces ask for human co-operation in diffusing a
rational understanding of the relationship between the two
spheres; they earnestly implore scientific minds to set aside
prejudice and skepticism, which lead nowhere, and co-operate
by establishing institutions for careful, unbiased research,
centers to which ignorant spirits can be brought and enlightened from the mortal side."

Wickland had organized The National Psychological Institute, mentioned in his dialogue with Houdini, for this purpose. He described it as "a benevolent association to carry on
experimental research in normal and abnormal psychology as
a nucleus to disseminate knowledge relating to the problem of
Life and Death and the Science of Religion." He hoped that
"the fact of survival will ultimately be placed on a rational,
scientific basis, proving 'It is not all of life to live, nor all of
death to die.' "

The Wickland method illustrates to us, today, why the kind
of mediumship practiced by Anna Wickland did not, after
all, provide the "rational, scientific" data scholars demand
and seek. A man as well-trained and strong-minded as Dr.
Wickland came to his ideas on the basis of personal experiences, of which one, during his formative professional years,
is particularly striking.

During his initial surgery training, Wickland dissected
human bodies. One morning he left for the hospital with no
intention of doing any dissecting. However, he and other
medical students were given the task of dissecting the lower
part of a man's body. In the afternoon, Wickland had
to dissect a lower limb. When he came home, he found Anna
staggering around the house. As he put his hand on her
shoulder, a spirit appeared to take control of Wickland's wife
and said, "What do you mean by cutting me?" Wickland

answered that he wasn't cutting anyone, but the entity replied, "Of course you are. You are cutting my leg."

An argument ensued between Wickland and the spirit entity, which ended with the spirit's demand for chewing tobacco or, at least, a pipe. In fact, the entity was later quoted by Wickland—a man, on the basis of his writings, not much given to humor—as saying, "I am dying for a smoke." Wickland's account states that the spirit eventually "realized his true condition and left." Later, checking the medical history of the man whose body he had dissected, the fledgling physician found that he had been an inveterate tobacco user.

The incident can, presumably, be explained by telepathy (Anna Wickland was reading her husband's mind, including the image of the dissected leg) and clairvoyance (the medium gained the knowledge of the man's smoking habit by ESP); but one can't really blame young Wickland for being shocked and impressed by such an incident, and to adopt his own Spiritualist version of life after death, education of "ignorant spirits" and healing, by exorcism, of spirit-possessed men and women.

17. Let Us Live and Die
as if We Were Immortal!

Those who seem to have passed beyond death, but return to tell about their experience, say that their impressions are essentially indescribable. And how, even on the basis of our own daily limited life experiences could it be any different? We have a difficult enough time understanding other ethnic groups, cultural patterns, geographic conditions—surely, any life dimension beyond our own must be difficult or impossible to describe. Language has limitations, as well as nuances that have nothing to do with words and syntax. A poet may use rhythms or associated sounds to convey meanings that elude a rational stringing-together of mere words. An orator can, using his voice like an instrument, arouse emotions within his audience that have no relation to the actual meaning of his words; even irrational or incoherent oratory can inspire feelings and actions that exceed the impact of rational argument.

It is only natural, therefore, that, as Dr. Raymond Moody has found, the near-death or beyond-death experience is ineffable, indescribable. The British psychical researcher, Mrs. Rosalind Heywood, unique because she is both an expressive writer and medium, once said of a mystical experience that describing it would be "like trying to reproduce the Matthew Passion on a tin lid with a spoon." It is the better part of wisdom, therefore, to assume quite simply that there are things we cannot understand, cannot describe, and cannot imagine. Religious figures, philosophers, socalled spirit entities and mystics of various types have given us descriptions of that unimaginable dimension: life after death.

I, frankly, do not care much for any one of them. I do not care, at heart, whether there are seven or eighteen or twenty-three additional spiritual states that we may experience as we pass from one after-life state to a higher one. I cannot comprehend the supposed roles, interrelationships and levels of position of assorted earth-bound spirits, nature-spirits, angelic, demonic or diabolic entities, of "spirit-healing groups," or of the various forms of rebirth, transmigration of the soul, of the possibility, likelihood or desirability of reincarnation. Nor do I understand, after much study, how existence between death and rebirth might work out, or how spirit entities might be split-offs or recombinations of personalities from our own level of existence. A case can be made for all of these hypotheses and for the information sources on which they are based. But there is a good deal of contradiction among them, and I personally do not see why I should have to accept or adopt any one of them.

· And yet, of course, we are all curious about an after-life and wonder, "What will it be like?"

Will we recognize one another, as the out-of-the-body and deathbed experiences suggest? And will we not only meet the family members we love, and who love us, but also antagonists, even enemies from previous incarnations? Will victims meet their murderers, and vice versa? What is the shadow side of the nether world? Going to Heaven, to sing God's praise may be to some a worth-while aim; but can God really desire eternal sycophancy? Like so much else, it is beyond my imaginings; and surely, beyond those of many, many others.

Our curiosity must, I feel, be curbed; it must stop, so to speak at the water's edge—one of the symbolic images that is part of the near-death experience. We can go so far, and no further, either in our imagination, or speculation, or in the type of investigative experiment that modern life-beyond-death studies entail. There is a distinct point at which our individual and collective minds cannot break through the pattern of their limited capacities. Let us respect the vast void beyond ourselves.

Nor need we, with all the information we now have, look upon death with an expectation of kindliness. True, the symbol of the Grim Reaper, even the phrase that "the wages of sin, its many guises and temptations—always with Death as wallowed in self-denial, that wagged its tongues to speak of sin, its many guises and tempatations—always with Death as the ultimate punishment. It is rather difficult to accept the view, brought back by the witnesses of life-after-death, that a rosy glow prevails "on the other side" (Spiritualists used to speak of it as "the summerland"), when the concept of Mortal Sin still hangs like a theological cloud over much of mankind.

There is much common sense sentiment against prolonging human life beyond a certain point. The idea of death with dignity is gaining ground. But this need not mean that we must look forward to death, just because some current research has given us a new view of it. Scientists in the field have had odd suggestions from people who have become fascinated with the potential of such research. Overly enthusiastic volunteers have even offered to commit suicide, "if it will help your research." Here, too, there is a point at which research-for-research's sake must draw a line. Surely, it is all right to accept, and even welcome, death when its time has truly come, when what we call life is simply not worth prolonging by the extraordinary means which medical technology has developed. But I still listen with compassion to the words written by the late Welsh poet, Dylan Thomas, addressed to his aging father: "Do not go gentle into that good night, Old age should burn and rave at close of day; Rage, rage, against the dying of the light."

Neither birth nor death are easy. And all our life is a fight for survival, because every defeat, setback or hunger pang is a signal, a messenger from death. Where, then, do we stand? We stand, I suggest, precisely where we have stood for all the thousands of years on which there is a record. At the beginning of this book, I referred to the Epic of *Gilgamesh*, pieced together from Babylonian tablets and most probably going back to a Sumerian oral tradition that dates the epic some three thousand years before the birth of Christ, or 5,000 years before our own era.

And what does it tell us? It describes the bewilderment of King Gilgamesh, whose one-time antagonist and later friend, Enkidu, dies in the fullness of youthful strength. The epic poem is magnificently introspective, bitter, questioning, defiant and eventually quiescent. It illustrate's man's essentially unchanged puzzlement over the very existence of death. As he is dying, Enkidu speaks to Gilgamesh, telling him that he will be "alone and wander," while "looking for the life that's gone" or "some eternal life you have to find." One can even find a parallel in the near death experiences of which we hear today, in his words, "My pain is that my eyes and ears / No longer hear and see the same / As yours do. Your eyes have changed." And then, the eternal question, "Why am I to die; You to wander alone?" The passage concludes: "Gilgamesh sat hushed at his friend's eyes stilled. / In his silence he reached out / To touch the friend whom he had lost."

How much of what you have read in the case histories in this book, and other books, is a reflection of hope against hope, of wishful thinking, of the desperate smile which masks fear and desperation? I honestly do not know. I only know that people must have hope, or they might kill their children at birth. Surely, some of us, seeing a loved one suffering on his or her deathbed, would—if we only had the courage and did not fear it as a sin or crime—go and strangle them with our bare hands; or, as they now say in the electronic Intensive Care Units, "pull the plug"? How torn we are! How fearful! And how often do we not know that we are lying, if only to ourselves, about our own death expectations and about the death of others?

All this, I grant you, does not echo the optimism, the new hope, the promise of Eternal Life that permeates many of the preceding pages. But at the closing of a book like this, there is a time for facing basic questions humbly, but without hesitation. Death is a nettle to be grasped. Because, death forces us to answer the essential questions of life itself. And here are some of them:

Is this all there is to it? It this all: this frustrated child, aimless adolescent, beleaguered adult, neglected "senior citizen"? Birth, suffering and death.

These questions come down on us with the persistence of a hailstorm on the roof. As we have lost the equanimity of accepting things as they are, because that's the way they have always been, our daily life is in ferment. Children are expected to set their own educational pattern. Young men and women search for "meaningful" occupations and find them scarce. Couples are being bombarded with slogans about "open marriage" and other sexual experimentation. Our society questions its own values and structures, finds corruption and crime where it had hoped to see integrity. Government is under a moral siege.

These are not theoretical questions, being asked of something abstract, known as "society." These are questions concerning our own individual worth and existence. Why was

I born? Because my parents made a quick decision, or none at all? Must I have children, in a world overcrowded with people? Do I live to work and make money, although my work adds to pollution, devours energy, and my savings melt away with inflation? Must my life be prolonged, though I may suffer, by medical technology? Will I die in confusion, in agony, a burden to myself and others?

Is that all there is to it? Are we just like maggots, on an apple called earth, or creatures headed for extinction, like so many mammoths?

Indeed, indeed, life would have more obvious meaning, would give us greater incentive for living, for maturing, if we could be sure of that one ultimate great aim: life beyond death—if there's a continuity that makes our existence on this earth a corridor leading to other forms of existence. The Reverend Jon Mundy, in his book *Learning to Die* (Evanston, 1973) said that we do not know "whether death may not even turn out to be the greatest of blessings." This, of course, is one hope we hardly dare to express: although, in our forgivable ignorance, it is as valid as any other hope or fear.

If we anticipate the death of those we love, if we think of making their dying an easier path, or even the road to "the greatest of blessings," then we might as well proceed on the assumption that death is not the end. Once we get away from the idea of death as punishment, eternity looks bright beyond our imagination. Why not, indeed, assume immortality as fact? It has much going for it, including our innermost needs, hopes and half-certainties. I have given up thinking, despite the evidence presented in this book, that modern science will find totally convincing proof either for or against a survival of the human personality after death. When the Society for Psychical Research was founded in London, more than a century ago, its leading minds sought a scientific basis for traditional religious belief; that was their original motivation for founding the Society. But in the intervening century, even now with our new technology, their quest stands out for its courage and force; still, none of the survival research has satisfied strict laboratory and experimental demands.

Looking back, we see the nineteenth century as a century of hope and high expectation. Our own, while not a century of despair, is nevertheless one of severe self-criticism, of shocked comprehension of man's limited potential. Although science fails us on the question of survival after death, the hypothesis of immortality remains the very best there is. Just because we may not, in our own century, achieve laboratory proof of survival—that does not mean survival is not real!

Living in awareness of death is not a research enterprise. In fact, science in its more tedious and thus respectable guises, has really no business in the shadow or light of death; at best, it is a tolerated intruder, only potentially helpful. If we act and talk as if survival after death were a known fact, we do no more than admit the obvious: that we are ignorant, and know it; but that we are also optimistic and courageous. Most of life goes on with a great "As If" governing it. "As If" our individual person were really important. "As If" our tasks were truly worthwhile. And: "As If" we were immortal . . .

At the outset of this book, I quoted Fyodor Dostoevsky as writing that "the concept of immortality" is "the single supreme idea on earth." Even more passionately, the poet Alfred Lord Tennyson has shouted, "If there is no immortality, I shall hurl myself into the sea." Poets are the guardians and voices of our souls. Dylan Thomas and Tennyson challenge religious faith just as they do scientific faith and performance.

What, then, do we need at this point? It is, surprisingly enough, kindness. It is a kindness to be displayed, first of all, toward ourselves, and toward our families and friends. With that as a base, we can show and practice kindness toward others. Such kindness is the very opposite of impatience and harsh demands—again, both towards ourselves and others. Kindness is the feeling, the word, the look that assumes the very best in our attitude toward life and death. It suggests that today's wrinkle, slow gait or illness does not indirectly signal a destructiveness that assumes death to be—I know it sounds silly—a dead end street. Kindness is, in a low key, the ultimate of positive assumption: that this is, indeed, not all there is to it; that we have important tasks to fulfill right here, in this life, and to the best our ability; but we may also assume these to be only steps on a much longer path that we cannot perceive.

Evidence of a world beyond is, as we have seen, vast, various, and at times confusing. Deathbed observations, visions, mystical experiences, séance room phenomena, out-of-the-body experiences, apparitions, spontaneous and laboratory phenomena—all these are hints that tantalize, seem to convince, suggest another reality, but leave us within our own dimensions most of the time.

That, I presume, is as it should be. Anything beyond intimations of immortality might be too much for us to bear, or to integrate into our limited understanding. But if we have faith, let us hold on to it. I we have belief, let us examine the evidence that may confirm that belief. If we have evidence, let us not ignore it. But, by all means, let us live and die as if we were immortal.

Suggested Reading

The literature on life after death is extensive and varied. In addition to sources cited in the body of this book, the reader may want to study other works, and the following listing should act as a guide in this direction. Probably the most professional bibliographical source book in this and related fields is Parapsychology: Sources of Information, *compiled under the auspices of the American Society for Psychical research by Rhea A. White and Laura A. Dale (Metuchen, N.J.: Scarecrow Press, 1973), a carefully organized and well annotated volume.*

Barrett, Sir William, *Death-Bed Visions.* London: Methuen, 1926.
Crookall, Robert, *Casebook of Astral Projection,* New Hyde Park, N.Y.: University Books, 1972.
————, *The Interpretation of Cosmic & Mystical Experiences,* London: James Clarke, 1969.
————, *Intimations of Immortality,* London: James Clarke, 1965.
————, *The Jung-Jaffé View of Out-of-the-Body Experiences,* World Fellowship Press, 1970.
————, *The Mechanisms of Astral Projection,* Moradabad, India: Darshana International, 1968.
————, *More Astral Projections,* London: Aquarian Press, 1964.
————, *Out-of-the-Body Experiences: A Fourth Analysis,* New Hyde Park, N.Y.: University Books, 1970.
————, *The Study and Practice of Astral Projection,* London: Aquarian Press, 1961.
————, *The Supreme Adventure,* London: James Clarke, 1961.
————, *The Techniques of Astral Projection,* London: Aquarian Press, 1964.
Ducasse, C. J., *The Belief in a Life after Death.* Springfield, Ill.: Charles C Thomas, 1961.
Ebon, Martin, *They Knew the Unknown.* New York: World Publishing Co., 1971.
Feifel, Herman (ed.), *The Meaning of Death.* New York: McGraw-Hill, 1959.

Green, Celia, *Out-of-the-Body Experiences*. Oxford: Inst. of Psychophysical Research, 1968.

Greenhouse, Herbert B., *The Astral Journey*. Garden City, N.Y., 1975.

Gurney, Edmund; Myers, F. W. H.; Podmore, Frank, *Phantasms of the Living*. London: Trübner, 1886.

Hart, Hornell, *The Enigma of Survival*. Springfield, Ill.: Charles C. Thomas, 1959.

Hocking, William E., *The Meaning of Immortality*. New York: Harper, 1957.

Hyslop, James H., *Psychical Research and the Resurrection*. Boston: Small, Maynard, 1908.

Jaffé, Aniela, *Apparitions and Precognition*. New Hyde Park, N.Y.: University Books, 1963.

Kübler-Ross, Elisabeth (ed.), *Death: The Final Stage of Growth*. Englewood Cliffs, N.J.: Prentice-Hall, 1975.

Monroe, Robert, *Journeys Out of the Body*. Garden City, N.Y.: Doubleday, 1971.

Moody, Raymond, *Life after Life*. New York: Bantam Books, 1976.

———, *Reflections on Life after Life*. Covington, Ga., and New York: Mockingbird/Bantam, 1977.

Muldoon, Sylvan, and Carrington, Hereward, *The Phenomena of Astral Projection*. London: Rider, 1951.

Murphy, Gardner, *Challenge of Psychical Research: A Primer of Parapsychology*. New York: Harper, 1961.

Myers, F. W. H., *Human Personality and its Survival of Bodily Death*. London: Logmans, 1903.

Osis, Karlis, *Deathbed Observations by Physicians and Nurses*. New York: Parapsychology Foundation, 1961.

Osis, Karlis, and Haraldsson, Erlendur, *At the Hour of Death*. New York: Avon, 1977.

Saltmarsh, H. F., *Evidence of Personal Survival from Cross-Correspondences*. London: Society for Psychial Research, 1938.

Smith, Susy, *Life Is Forever*. New York: G. P. Putnam's, 1974.

———, *The Enigma of Out-of-the-Body Travel*. New York: Garrett Publications, 1965.

Toynbee, Arnold (and others), *Man's Concern with Death*. New York: McGraw-Hill, 1968.

Tyrrell, G. N. M., *Apparitions*. London: Society for Psychical Research, 1953.

About the Author

Martin Ebon served for twelve years as Administrative Secretary of the Parapsychology Foundation and subsequently as a consultant to the Foundation for Research on the Nature of Man. He conducted a series of lectures on "Parapsychology: From Magic to Science" at the New School for Social Research in New York City and has lectured widely, throughout the United States, at institutes of higher learning. Mr. Ebon has edited such periodicals as *Tomorrow*, the *International Journal of Parapsychology*, and *Spiritual Frontiers*, organ of the Spiritual Frontiers Fellowship.

Mr. Ebon's articles and reviews have appeared in a variety of periodicals, ranging from *Contemporary Psychology* to the *U.S. Naval Institute Proceedings*. More than twenty of his books have been published by NAL alone. Among them are PROPHECY IN OUR TIME, THEY KNEW THE UNKNOWN, MAHARISHI: THE FOUNDER OF TRANSCENDENTAL MEDITATION, and TM: HOW TO FIND PEACE OF MIND THROUGH MEDITATION.

SIGNET Books of Related Interest

☐ **MANY MANSIONS by Gina Cerminara.** The most convincing proof of reincarnation and ESP ever gathered in one volume. A trained psychologist's examination of the files and case histories of Edgar Cayce, the greatest psychic of our time. (#E7736—$1.75)

☐ **THE WORLD WITHIN by Gina Cerminara.** An adult, credible, and inspiring book that frankly faces the realities of twentieth century living in dealing with the implications of reincarnation by the author of **Many Mansions.** (#Y5996—$1.25)

☐ **MANY LIVES, MANY LOVES by Gina Cerminara.** In this thought-provoking sequel to **Many Mansions** and **The World Within,** Gina Cerminara fully explains the theory of reincarnation and the meaning it has for present-day lives. Strong evidence is presented through the recorded experiences of such well-known psychics as Edgar Cayce and Peter Hurkos. (#W6112—$1.50)

☐ **ARTHUR FORD: The Man Who Talked With the Dead by Allen Spraggett with William V. Rauscher.** Allen Spraggett, a leading psychic researcher, probes the extraordinary powers of the sensational medium who lived in two worlds. (#W5804—$1.50)

☐ **UNKNOWN BUT KNOWN: My Adventure into the Meditative Dimension by Arthur Ford.** Arthur Ford, a psychic researcher and pioneer thinker, explains his philosophy and gives us ways in which we can communicate with the other world. (#Q5296—95¢)

Other SIGNET Books You Will Want to Read

☐ **NEW WORLDS OF THE UNEXPLAINED by Allen Spraggett.** The astonishing, true-life experiences of people who have crossed over that invisible boundary into the unknown. . . . (#W6876—$1.50)

☐ **ADVENTURES INTO THE PSYCHIC by Jess Stearn.** A fully documented account of every major aspect of the occult field today, it takes the reader through a series of psychic experiences, ranging from ESP, seances, and telepathic crime detection. (#W7822—$1.50)

☐ **YOUR MYSTERIOUS POWERS OF ESP by Harold Sherman.** Telepathy, extrasensory healing, communications with the dead, out-of-body travel—unlock the secrets of your own amazing psychic sensitivity and learn how to make ESP a more dynamic part of your everyday life. (#Y6916—$1.25)

☐ **MASTERING THE TAROT: Basic Lessons in an Ancient, Mystic Art by Eden Gray.** Unlock the secrets of the tarot. Learn to understand their mysterious and beautiful symbols. Fully illustrated. (#W6131—$1.50)

☐ **THE COMPLETE ILLUSTRATED BOOK OF DIVINATION AND PROPHECY by Walter B. Gibson & Litzka R. Gibson.** Tarot cards, i ching, hand of fate, palmistry, playing-card forecasting, and many other methods of prophesying your future have been gathered in one volume, together with explanatory charts and diagrams and a glossary of divination, to make foretelling the future easier. (#E6525—$2.25)

EVOKE

THE

WISDOM

OF

THE

TAROT

With your own set of 78, full-color cards—the Rider-Waite deck you have studied in **THE TAROT REVEALED.**

ORDER FORM